# QUEEN ANNE'S REVENGE

## CS-405: BOOK ONE

## BLAZE WARD

**Queen Anne's Revenge**
**CS-405: Book One**
Blaze Ward
Copyright © 2019 Blaze Ward
All rights reserved
Published by Knotted Road Press
www.KnottedRoadPress.com

ISBN: 978-1-64470-006-8

Cover art:

ID 63735258 © Algol | Dreamstime.com
ID 2880466 © Kurt Tutschek | Dreamstime.com

Cover and interior design © 2019 Knotted Road Press

**Never miss a release!**
If you'd like to be notified of new releases, sign up for my newsletter.

I only send out newsletters once a quarter, will never spam you, or use your email for nefarious purposes. You can also unsubscribe at any time.

http://www.blazeward.com/newsletter/

**The Jessica Keller Chronicles**

*Auberon*

*Queen of the Pirates*

*Last of the Immortals*

*Goddess of War*

*Flight of the Blackbird*

*The Red Admiral*

*St. Legier*

**CS-405**

*Queen Anne's Revenge*

*Packmule*

*Persephone*

**Additional Alexandria Station Stories**

*The Story Road*

*Siren*

*Two Bottles of Wine with a War God*

**The Science Officer Series**

*The Science Officer*

*The Mind Field*

*The Gilded Cage*

*The Pleasure Dome*

*The Doomsday Vault*

*The Last Flagship*

*The Hammerfield Gambit*

*The Hammerfield Payoff*

**Doyle Iwakuma Stories**

*The Librarian*

*Demigod*

*Greater Than The Gods Intended*

**Other Science Fiction Stories**

*Myrmidons*

*Moonshot*

*Menelaus*

*Earthquake Gun*

*Moscow Gold*

*Fairchild*

*White Crane*

***The Collective* Universe**

*The Shipwrecked Mermaid*

*Imposters*

# TROUBLE (APRIL 3, 402)

COMMAND CENTURION PHIL KOSNETT didn't figure he'd been asleep long. Just enough to get all the way to the bottom when an alert signal jolted him back awake.

It took several seconds for his brain to follow him out of the dream, time he took cataloging the volume around himself, looking for coherence. *CS-405*, his Corvette/Scout. Phil was in his cabin. Picture of his wife Xui Yi on the wall, with both kids' latest school pics below that.

Why was there a red tinge to the lights?

His comm chirped a second time, snapping him fully awake. He reached out a hand and poked the button.

"Kosnett," he more or less growled, still a little surly from deep sleep.

"Lau," his first officer replied simply. She had the deck while he got everyone back to a normal watch rotation. "We have a problem."

Phil exploded out of his bunk, keying the lights to full and looking for his tunic. Heather Lau was one of the best officers he had ever served with, in seventeen years active duty. She never raised unnecessary alarms.

"Be there in five," Phil said aloud, stuffing his left foot into a slipper while he got an arm into his tunic. "What happened?"

"We just lost both JumpSails," she replied in a hard, angry voice. "Explosion and fire in Engineering. Rushforth is shutting systems down, but we're dead in space right now."

"How far did we make it?" Phil asked, finally getting to the door to his cabin and unlocking the door.

"Roughly forty light hours out from *Severnaya Zemlya*," came the reply after a moment to check her figures. Heather always double checked her figures. "We should be safe for a bit, but we're still way behind enemy lines."

Phil considered the situation for a moment, staring at his favorite picture of Xui Yi and wondering if he might never make it home to her. It was always an occupational hazard in the *Republic of Aquitaine* Navy. Even more so when you served with First Expeditionary Fleet, currently a thousand light years inside *Buran* space.

"You keep command," Phil said. "I'll go down and help Rushforth. If Chief Battenhouse isn't awake, roust him and send him my way. Maintain red alert for now and have Siobhan take over as Tactical Officer."

"On it," she said, cutting the line.

Bad time to happen, but a good Command Centurion was always looking for opportunities to train his crew. Heather was going to be his peer soon, probably with the next command slot that opened up on this front. She should get comfortable with the idea.

Of course, if the fire was as bad as it could be, they might all end up in a prison camp.

Well, most of them.

Fleet Centurion Keller had reminded everyone of the standing orders for Command Centurions facing imminent capture.

If that happened, Phil Kosnett was expected to go down with his ship.

# ENGINEERING (APRIL 3, 402)

PHIL CLEARED the fifth frame hatch and could suddenly smell a tinge of smoke in the air of the aft-running corridor. Not bad enough to set off more alarms, or maybe Chief Engineer Rushforth had overridden them to keep the noise from getting on everyone's nerves. She was like that.

There was a group of sailors in the hallway, just this side of the next frame hatch. Phil moved to join them. He recognized the squat figure of Bok Battenhouse from behind, standing next to the Chief Engineer, Kamila Rushforth. The Boatswain was almost as broad as he was tall, all shoulders, muscles, and long arms on a frame barely one hundred and seventy centimeters tall. In spite of being nearly a head taller than the Boatswain, Phil figured the gray-headed Chief still outweighed him.

As Phil stepped closer, Kam was issuing orders to a group of men and women in protective clothing and life support masks. She nearly smacked Phil in the face as he came up behind her, but he decided not to tease her about talking more with her hands than her mouth. That could wait until later.

"Okay, step four," she was saying in a hard, authoritative voice, glancing back at him but not including Phil in the conversation. "Janowski, manually close up and check any air vents still open and then make sure all your people are clear. When you give me the signal, I'll vent the entire space once hard, hold it for five minutes, and then you'll have to go in with skinsuits to make sure all the louvers open up again so we can repressurize things. Questions?"

"Negative," the other woman, Janowski, said. "Confirming channel four for the team?"

"Channel four," the engineer said.

Phil watched without comment as Janowski led the other three firefighters to the hatch, popped it open, and then moved through quickly. A puff of smoke came the other direction like a djinni summoned from the bottle, except this one wasn't about to offer Phil wishes.

Rushforth stepped to the hatch and sealed it from this side, leaving just the two of them, with Battenhouse close by. She took the time to make sure the seal was solid before she finally turned to face him.

Everything Kamila Rushforth did was careful and deliberate, in contrast to her name. She never rushed anywhere.

"Phil," she said with a sharp nod.

"Status?" he asked.

One of the joys of this crew for Phil, and having so many people trying to get into any open slots with this fleet, was that his people were much better than average, at worst. Kamila Rushforth was better than most. At thirty-three, she was already a Chief Engineer and would probably be on a cruiser when the next slot opened.

It was nice, being able to expect excellence from his people as a matter of course.

She nodded once as a placeholder.

"We've shut down oxygen inside and flooded all the spaces with pure nitrogen once we accounted for crew members," she said, biting the words off.

She wasn't angry at him. Possibly at the gods that had chosen her ship to suffer an explosion. Combat was like that. Six hours ago, they had made the jump out from *Severnaya Zemlya*, having strafed the Starbase there in passing, as part of one of Jessica Keller's most audacious raids yet.

And then something failed. Things like that happened in combat and the immediate aftermath. It just happened to be *CS-405* that took the hit.

"Casualties?" Phil asked, bracing himself.

These would be people he knew. Faces that made up the two hundred and seven names of his crew.

"Two confirmed dead, eight injured," she said. "A couple bad enough they might not make it."

"I'll let the Surgeon handle that," Phil replied. "I can't do anything but get in his way right now. What do you need here?"

"Nothing at the moment, sir," she answered. "If this works, we'll snuff the fire out and freeze any hot spots. I've shut down the rear generators and all the engines as well. We can run on the forward array and batteries for a few hours, assuming we don't have to fight."

"This corvette is a scout, Kam," he said, his own voice hard. "If we have to fight anything bigger than a pocket freighter, we're in way worse trouble."

"Hang on," she said, putting one hand up to her ear. Her eyes lost focus. "Okay, Janowski. Confirming that everyone is safe and accounted for. Stand by for hard vacuum."

As Phil watched, she moved to a screen on the port wall and called up a new board. She typed several commands and then turned back to him.

"I need a second senior officer's approval to vent

engineering," she announced. "Was planning to call Heather, but you're here."

Phil moved to the board and entered a password on the second line of the override screen. The hallway abruptly filled with a siren that would have woken him completely up earlier, unlike the comm that just broke his sleep.

"Chief," Kam said, finally acknowledging the old man remaining with them. "My people are going to be on that generator and the JumpSails. Have all your Damage Control teams running everything else down until we know where we're at."

"On it, Kam," Bok said, grabbing his own comm from his belt and moving a little ways off so he could talk to his folks.

The man who was the Boatswain, senior enlisted man aboard, was sixty-two years old, and had served in the Navy continuously for forty-one years. There wasn't much he hadn't seen or done in his time. Bok wasn't an officer today because he didn't want to be one, not because he wouldn't have been damned good at it.

"Is there anything I can do?" Phil asked.

Again, good people, intent on doing a good job. All he generally had to do was point them at a problem and get the hell out of the way. Or let them work when the problem found them.

"Keep killer robots off my ass while I fix the Jump system, boss," Kam said. "Won't know any more than that until I get in there and start taking things apart."

"Roger that," Phil said. "Send me occasional updates when you have news."

And then he walked away. His Chief Engineer and Boatswain had the technical stuff in hand. Either they could fix it, or they couldn't.

His job was figuring out what they did next.
And how many people would make it home.
Next stop: Medbay.

# MEDICAL (APRIL 3, 402)

THE MEDBAY WAS a madhouse when Phil arrived. For a crew of two hundred and seven, they had one Surgeon and two nurses, plus a variety of crewmembers with some level of medical training. It felt like everyone who wasn't on a Damage Control team or on duty was down here, sewing, gluing, inspecting, or otherwise helping. Just a different kind of damage control.

Phil stopped at the open door and surveyed the chaos, rather than wading in. The room was standing room only. A familiar face was working on a patient close by.

"Max," Phil said, drawing the Nursing Tech Yeoman's eyes up. "Status?"

The man took a deep breath and kept cleaning a wound that was slowly dripping blood onto the metal floor. His eyes seemed far away for a moment, and then they snapped back to the present.

"Three dead, Commander," Max said. "Doc Hanley's got the last one in surgery with Andre assisting. Got one stable at critical right now. I've got the walking wounded. What do you need?"

"That's all, Yeoman," Phil said. "Tell Hanley I dropped by when he gets out, and let him know that we're dead in space, so I can't make a high-speed run back to the station to get him help."

The man Max was working on started to move, to rise.

"I should be back there helping," he said, trying to withdraw the wounded arm. "You can sew this up later."

Max surprised both of them by coming out of his squat and shoving the larger engineer bodily back into the chair.

"You can do that when I'm done with you," Max growled. "Sit down."

Another surprise. Yeoman Max Bathurst was a slender man of average build, giving up something like ten centimeters and ten kilos to the bigger engineer, First-Rate-Spacer Markus Dunklin. The extra mass hadn't helped him one bit with the smaller man.

"Commander?" Dunklin asked for help.

"You heard the man, Dunklin," Phil said. "Get the arm cleaned and glued first. You can head aft only after Max releases you. Boatswain and Chief Engineer will be at it for a while."

"Aye, sir," Dunklin subsided. "Will do."

"Thank you, Commander," Max said as he went back to scanning the wound for any more fragments to remove.

"Thank you, Max," Phil said. "I'm just glad you have everything under control here."

He exited. Doc Hanley didn't need him interrupting a surgery to say anything that Max hadn't been able to convey.

Plus, he had what he needed. The ship was wounded. The crew as well. But both could overcome that, once he figured out how to get them out of enemy space and home.

# BRIDGE (APRIL 4, 402)

Phil had pulled his top two officers into the small day-office off the bridge so they could talk privately. It was the place where the officer of the deck could do paperwork in semi-seclusion, still not more than a moment away from any crew needs. Not that they had anything that needed to be kept from the crew, but the officers would be in damage control on the humans around here as well as the steel for a while. Best to keep things contained for now.

Senior Centurion Heather Lau was his Executive Officer. She handled everything Tactical when they were in combat. A long, slender woman with equally-long, black hair, she always appeared to be taller than she was, until you got close enough to realize that those bright, green eyes weren't at your level. They just felt that way at times. Like his Chief Engineer, he expected to lose Lau as soon as a slot opened up, for Heather to take command of another corvette. As long as it was with First Expeditionary Fleet.

He could see Heather turning down a command back home on a quiet frontier. She wasn't one of the angry warriors like Alber' d'Maine accumulated on *VI Victrix*, but she would want a war posting. That much he knew.

And where Heather was tall and pale, his Second Officer was short, with brown skin so dark it almost looked black in the right light and curly hair she normally kept buzzed tight against her skull. Would need to do it again in a few days.

Siobhan Skokomish was still more of a quiet introvert in most things than Heather, a nav officer who did complicated math problems in her head. But like the Chief Engineer, never a wasted movement in her calm deliberation.

"Should the Engineer be here?" Heather asked as they sat.

"No," Phil said. "I need her and the Boatswain fixing things. What do we know for certain?"

"I had Siobhan review the logs of the run on that station yesterday," Heather said. "We had the van on the port side, leading in *VI Victrix*. After they woke up, the station poured all their available fire into Denis Jež and *Vanguard*, with a few shots into the escorts and almost nothing aimed at the three cruisers."

"And I was jamming them with everything I had," Siobhan added. "They only got four solid hits on us. Shield caught two with a little bit of leakage. The other two hit metal, but we were running away full tilt on both. Glancing shots at extreme range."

"Yes," Phil agreed. "Nothing on the Damage Control reports looked bad. Mostly armor and hull systems. Do we know what caused that generator to overload?"

"Negative," Siobhan replied. "According to maintenance records, it was about mid-life to the next major service, and hadn't given us any issues before now."

"Okay, so we've made it clear from the attack, everything looked good at that point, and I went to bed," Phil said. "What happened next?"

"T-minus seventeen minutes, that generator started throwing odd errors," Heather took up the narrative again, checking her notes on a tablet on the table top in front of her. "Nothing bad, just starting to waver off zero by a few points. Other systems have behaved worse with no problems, and we had other complications we were sorting out, trying to make sure we hit rendezvous with the rest of the squadron."

"Siobhan?" Phil asked.

"Went through the error logs, Phil," she replied, brown eyes squinted at the memory. "Nothing jumped out at me, but I'm a pilot, not an engineer. Kam might be able to see something in all the noise."

"Make a note to have her team review everything when the current emergency is over," he ordered.

"Will do," Heather continued. "T-minus eight minutes, the errors suddenly spike hard. Chief Engineer was still on duty and moves to shut the generator down as it is suddenly well outside normal behavior and starts getting worse."

"Symptoms?" Phil asked.

"Combination of things," Siobhan said. "Control systems suddenly lost their minds, and a fuel line seems to have physically separated, releasing explosive gases into the generator's housing. Either would have been salvageable, but Kam couldn't see that the lines were still pumping hydrogen in, and couldn't get it to respond to a shut-down command. She orders one of the Damage Control teams into immediate action."

"How long did they take to respond?" Phil probed.

"First team was in place in five minutes, trying all the usual steps," Heather said. "That failed. Kam ordered them to just shut the thing down hard for now, until she could get a full engineering team prepped to take the generator apart. She still doesn't know she had a leak on her hands, because the sensors have stopped transmitting data outside their local array."

"Did one of the Damage Control people cause the explosion?" Phil asked in a hard voice.

"Negative," Heather was firm in her opinion. "They had just acknowledged the order to shut it down and were starting to open their toolboxes when the generator exploded, catching all five of them in a fireball and shockwave. Dominguez and Lee were killed immediately. Magone died later on the operating table. Ariana Trudeau is in critical but stable condition right now. El-Hashem is in serious condition. Dunklin returned to duty with his arm in a sling."

"Needs must when the devil drives," Phil quoted, acknowledging the hard-headed man getting his arm glued shut earlier. "So, explosion and fire, contained to engineering?"

"Affirmative, Phil," Heather said. "Everybody was already in air-gear, so Kam shut down oxygen as fast as she could confirm everybody was ready, but the feed line was already compromised. One of Boatswain's folks wrenched that line shut from the other end, shutting down most of the aft generators, Kam blew the atmosphere, and dropped the room to about forty degrees Absolute. Cold enough to freeze any fires. That's done, but we're dead in the water right now."

"Location?"

"Forty-three light hours out from *Severnaya Zemlya*," Siobhan replied. "Well south and in a relatively thin part of the outer system, so we won't run into anything, but we can't get back into JumpSpace until everything is repaired and tested. Kam says three to five days, best estimate."

"So we'll miss the rendezvous with Jessica?" Phil confirmed.

"Yes," Heather said. "Even if she waits over the normal deadline."

"Assume we're on our own then," he replied.

"A scout with no offensive firepower, a thousand light years behind enemy lines, with a broken JumpSail?" Siobhan asked.

"You joined the Navy for a challenge, right?" Phil asked.

# SCENE OF THE CRIME (APRIL 4, 402)

ANYBODY but the Boatswain doing it, and Kam would have insisted she be the one waist-deep in the shattered remnants of the auxiliary reactor, tracing lines and identifying potential issues. But Bok had literally been doing this since before she was born and had put his foot down.

She could have overridden his objections, but Bok had lost several of his people in the explosion and was taking this extremely personal.

At least they had managed to repair the damaged louvers and establish a good atmosphere in here. She couldn't imagine how hard this task would be in a lifesuit.

Bok's feet disappeared into the reactor housing as she watched. A moment later, his head appeared, probably standing on the port transverse bracing, to be eyeball level, with her squatting next to the device.

"It's a flipping mess down there, Kam," he said in a harsh growl.

"And?"

"Looks like the upper housing held when the line caught fire," he continued. "Expanding gases couldn't go up, so the pressure went down. I've got a couple of plates that look like torn paper down here."

"That's not good," she observed, prompting Bok to keep talking when his eyes got that far-away look.

"Worse, Kam," he said. "Looks like we vented into the underside of the JumpSail array. Metal there is deformed from heat."

"That would explain why we dropped into RealSpace," Kam said. "How bad is the damage?"

"We're going to need to pull the primary converter, both coolant systems, and probably a good chunk of the data cores, just to get underneath, but I can see soot here, so something organic fully oxidized."

"Okay, stand by," Kam said, grabbing the comm of her belt and keying channel six. "Ngo, this is Rushforth. Grab Dunklin and a toolbox. I need you to take apart the main JumpSail housing while we look at the reactor here. Higher priority than whatever else you're doing right now."

"Acknowledged," the man's voice came back. "Eight minutes while I get my lunch to go."

"Just shovel faster, Hossam," she said. "You'll be up late, so eating your food now is good."

Kam cut the line and picked up her engineering slab from the toolbox behind her where it had been waiting for her needs. Best place for it was between them on the deck, so she dropped it there and keyed the holo-projector.

She could see what the reactor was supposed to look like, back when it had a top and a front, rather than ragged teeth where it had spalled off lethal fragments. On her left, the controllers for the JumpSails, the unit that this particular reactor normally powered in combat. Behind the broken machine, across a small corridor between massive columns of steel and power, the secondary JumpSail. The tiny one that was designed to be used in an absolute worst-case scenario.

Like now.

She called up a secondary menu and reviewed the current damage status of everything, according to her team and all the sensors they had available.

There. Not even in the top twenty things to fix, by priority. That would need to change, if the main JumpSails were as badly damaged as Bok thought.

She had been unconsciously assuming that the shockwave just jarred things loose and they could patch it all up in a day. She changed the priority for repairs to the secondary JumpSail to number three and updated the list.

Bok must have been reading her mind. He was already climbing out of the well when she looked up. Kam grabbed the toolbox and her slab and stepped back.

"This is going to be a long journey," he said as he stood up next to her.

They were the same height, but Bok probably massed double what she did. Power wrenches would offset his advantage, but sometimes you had to get under a pry-bar and try to move the world. Bok was good at that.

"Why, so, Chief?" Kam asked.

"In my entire career, I've only been on a ship that had to use the secondary JumpSail one time, Kam," he replied. "Back on the old destroyer *Paramaribo*. About the time you were born."

"And it wasn't pleasant, Chief?" she asked, following as he set out. For a short man, he walked extremely fast. She had to hurry to keep up.

"Those boats were junk, Chief Engineer," he said over his shoulder. "Should have been sent to the wreckers about the time *I* was born. Navy didn't finally agree until about fifteen years ago, but at least *Paramaribo* was done after that. Lost the primary while out on patrol, clear down near the far border corner with *Lincolnshire*. Took us a month to limp to a port where we could get food and enough parts to make it to *Ramsey*. That got us enough parts and assistance to make it home, but a three-week shakedown cruise had us at sea for nearly four months. I don't even know what the closest friendly harbor is here."

"That's Phil's job," Kam said as he stopped and rested a possessive hand on the casing of the secondary drive.

Kam wondered if he was trying to read the state of the machine by osmosis or telepathy. You never knew with Bok, but he always seemed to know what was wrong with a device.

He turned to her now with a dark, heavy look in his eyes.

"Remind me to have a polite chat with that pirate fellow, Bedrov," he observed.

"Oh?" Kam raised an eyebrow.

Chief Battenhouse had never been one for port-side brawls, but that was the look on his face right now. A good, old-fashioned bar fight, usually over the slightest things.

"I agree with him that this particular layout is probably the most efficient use of space possible," Bok said with a nod. "But I think we need to shift the two JumpSails arrays to either ends of the Engineering spaces, with a frame between them, and add a second generator to handle the backups. This generator managed to kill both array controllers, one of them by melting the damned thing. This one was killed by a feedback surge over the electrical lines."

He squatted down and grabbed a power wrench from her toolbox as she called up the interior specs of the unit. Smaller than the main system by an order of magnitude. Barely big enough inside for a person, if you took out all the innards. Everything looked like wires and boards here, with just a few solid boxes.

Old design, going back centuries, probably, to when Baudin first invented the system. Too small to go fast, and probably too fragile to travel very far, but at RealSpace speeds, anything FTL was necessary if they wanted to get home.

"So you rewire everything here?" Kam asked. "If the lines are burned out?"

"That's what frightens me, Kam," Bok said as the first bolt backed out. "We could handle that part. Take maybe a week. Problem is, we've got nothing to calibrate it, so we have to throw ourselves into Jump, run for a while, then bounce out and spend a day or two figuring out where we landed."

"That's an engineering problem, Bok," she observed.

"Yeah, but we just blew up their damned Starbase back there, Kam," he said, attacking the second bolt. "Gonna be some very angry people out here looking for us while we're dinking around."

"Like I said earlier, Bok," she said. "That's Phil's job. Ours is to get the ship running again so he can get us there."

Unspoken, the implicit assumption that they could do that. Otherwise, they might have to open a direct beam signal back to *Severnaya Zemlya* and offer to surrender.

Assuming *Buran* took prisoners.

# WARDROOM (APRIL 4, 402)

SIOBHAN STOOD and waited for Centurion Gephardt to look up from his paperwork. They were in the mess hall, so it was public, but she thought it would be rude to just slide into the seat next to the man while he was figuring out meal schedules and his staff cleaned up everything from lunch.

Something caught his eye and he glanced up. A moment later he blushed. At least as much as a man with such light brown skin could.

Siobhan could blush all day long and nobody could tell, unless they saw her pupils. But she was from Dekoa, and that planet had been colonized almost exclusively by a diaspora from Central Africa on *Earth*, by way of *New Cameroon* and *Stokley*. Her skin could appear as polished onyx in the right light.

Julius Gephardt was from *Ballard*, and obviously related to the famous Iwakuma explorers, a mix of the best elements of Upper European Finns from *Earth* with the folks from *Zanzibar* that had been first to return to space after *The Darkness*. His skin was much lighter than hers, although not nearly as pale as the Euros or Chinese aboard. And he had inherited a beak of a nose from some Viking along the way.

Just none of their aggressiveness.

"Second Officer," he said formally with a nod.

Siobhan didn't take it personally. Julius retreated to formality when he got flustered.

And she knew she did that to him. If they didn't serve on the same ship, she might have considered flustering him more. Personally.

Instead, she dropped into the seat across from him. The slightly-more-formal one, as opposed to sitting right next to him where they might brush an arm.

He would probably explode with embarrassment, if she did that.

*Keep it simple, today. Don't flirt with him any more than usual. Maybe less. Don't think about maybe being captured or killed without talking to him about* things *first.*

"I wanted to talk to you about food stocks, Centurion," Siobhan replied, keeping things at least apparently formal for now. "What is our current status?"

Rather than reply, he pushed his slab across the table and spun it around so she could see the numbers. Like they would make any sense, listing tonnages and consumption rate calculations, from her quick glance down.

"As you can see," he apparently assumed she could absorb his chef's magic by smell, or something. "We can maintain current consumption for seventeen days until we have to break out the emergency meal packs stowed forward and on the flight deck."

Flight deck. Where you could, if you were lucky, be called on to stuff the meal packs into the administrative shuttle and send them off to some other poor bastard, somewhere else, and make him eat them, instead of you.

Siobhan had no interest in ever consuming oatmeal

again. Going down a uniform size, from sexy to scarecrow might rate higher.

"How much do we have in emergency rations?" she asked anyway, suspecting that much of the rest of the crew would feel the same way about stretching those stocks even further, by avoiding them altogether.

"Eleven days, assuming normal consumption," his sudden grin at her was a surprise. "I suspect this particular crew would probably manage sixteen without much complaining, as long as I didn't pay too close attention to the waste system overloads."

*Oh My God. Did he just tell a joke? In public? Without blushing?*

*There's hope for you yet, Jules.*

Siobhan smiled at his humor. The man was always too formal, but she knew that it was his introversion, rather than her presence. Anybody getting too close caused his walls to come up. She was just one of the few with the patience to use a version of Chinese-water-torture to bore a hole.

"So we could go roughly twenty-two to twenty-three days if we reduced caloric intake to three-quarters?" she asked.

"Twenty-seven, if we over-graze the hydroponics for vegetables and shrimp, and then reduce standards for unsafe food," he said, a smile suddenly lighting his face. "I would just have to add a bunch of cayenne to the diet, at that point. Teach you barbarians about real cooking. Maybe even make a jambalaya when you poor philistines are facing true starvation as an alternative."

Food was one of the few things that broke Julius out of his shell. Committing magic in the kitchen. She smiled back. His jambalaya was pretty-damned-good, but some of the folks on this crew might think they were supposed to strip industrial equipment with it, once they took a bite.

Plus, if they refused, she could have their share, and stay

that much farther away from the oatmeal. At least until starvation took hold. Anything but oatmeal.

"As Second Officer, you are hereby approved to make those choices necessary to stretch our food supplies as far as possible, Centurion," Siobhan said with a grin as she stood. "And maybe jambalaya."

He surprised her by standing as well and holding out a hand to shake.

Suddenly, she felt like she was part of a tiny conspiracy in the kitchen as they shook hands. Maybe it took the end of the world to bring Jules out of his shell?

She could live with that.

Anything, but oatmeal.

# VISITORS (APRIL 4, 402)

"ALERT," the voice came out of the speaker and had Phil halfway out of his seat, even as the lights turned red. "Emergence signature detected. All hands to battle stations."

Two steps and Phil was on the bridge itself, his paperwork on repair stocks already forgotten. Somewhere, Heather and Siobhan would be racing to their stations as well.

"How far away?" Phil asked as he threw himself into the station at the center of the room.

Old designs for destroyers had the command centurion at the aft end of the bridge, looking at the backs of heads. Phil liked this new thing, where everyone looked inward towards him from pairs of stations. He could see faces now.

The Yeoman on duty, Weston Lovisone, checked the boards and looked up again.

"Forty-nine light minutes, Commander," the man replied. "Looks like a small freighter from the signature, rather than a warship."

Phil said a small prayer of thanks to the god of JumpSails and the various goddesses of navigation systems. At that distance, anybody but another scout like them would be hard pressed to even spot *CS-405*, running as silent as possible in the night, let alone identify them. On the other hand, whoever it was might still see something and run, and there was nothing Phil could do about it right now.

"Engineering, this is the bridge," Phil called out, letting the systems route the call.

"Tuason here," a man's voice replied. "Chief Engineer and Boatswain are in the middle of something."

"Good enough, Galin," Phil said. "What's the status of jump?"

"That's what they're doing, sir," the engineering watch yeoman explained. "Primary's down until further notice. Backup is being taken apart now."

Inwardly, Phil cursed. Just about the worst timing he could imagine. Even those piss-poor excuses for starships that *Buran* used could outrun him right now.

"What about engines?" he asked.

"Stand by, Commander," Tuason said.

The line went silent.

Phil looked up as Siobhan came barreling through the hatch and almost jumped into the station next to Yeoman Lovisone.

"How are my engines?" she asked between heavy breaths. Must have run here from the forward end of the ship.

"Waiting to hear now," Phil replied.

She nodded and looked down, ignoring him while she got everything set up the way she wanted, and probably made sure nobody had touched anything. The woman was a perfectionist about her flying, even dead in space.

"Commander, this is Tuason," the engineer was back. "Kam says, and I quote '*Tell them they can start the engines, but don't let Siobhan do anything crazy yet.*' Unquote."

Phil chuckled at the sour look that drew from his pilot. She kept her opinions to herself, though, which was good.

"Acknowledged," Phil called instead. "Stand by for powered flight."

"Slowly, please?" Tuason added. "We're cold back there right now, so slamming it to the stops might break something."

"Will do, Tuason," Phil nodded to Siobhan. "Let Bok and Kam know."

Phil cut the line and glanced over at his Second Officer.

He could almost hear the grumbles from here, but they were probably only in her head. For now.

Still, he almost laughed out loud when she demurely pressed a single button on the screen with exaggerated care, like this was a training demonstration or something. Her eyeroll was just as perfect.

"Powered flight initiated," she said with enough sarcasm to polish steel. "Dead reckoning away. Do we have a course?"

"Negative, Pilot," Phil replied. "Get us moving away from them as quietly as we can."

The hatch opened a second time and the blond-haired man Phil wanted to see came through, still bleary-eyed. Phil did the math in his head and assumed Centurion Evan Brinich had been dead sound asleep when the alarm sounded. He was carrying slippers in one hand and his tunic in the other, dropping both in a pile by his station as he sat and quickly started pushing buttons.

Phil agreed with the man's assessment of the situation, even half asleep. Get to the bridge first, even in just an undershirt and pants. Get dressed later.

On his personal board, Heather Lau's face appeared at about the same time, coffee mug in hand, taking a sip. Knowing her, she had been in her cabin doing paperwork, but had made good time to the Emergency Bridge. And she wasn't nearly as tired-looking as Brinich.

Unlike other vessels, Phil Kosnett felt the place for the First Officer was forward, on the Emergency Bridge, where she could immediately take command if something happened to him aft on the Main Bridge. Too many times he had heard horror stories about ships that were suddenly crippled by a bridge hit taking out the entire command staff, or at least cutting off all communications, leaving command to devolve to a poor, junior Centurion who had been relegated to the posting equivalent of Siberia.

Phil juggled his officers and team around, moving someone every week so that everyone got a chance to work with everyone else. A ship this small needed to be a single family, trained and prepared. And for him that included serving with every officer and every enlisted until he knew how they were going to jump.

Little scout corvettes like this had four Type-1-Pulse beam emplacements, two fore and two aft. Fantastic for defense against missiles and fighters, and pretty good when *Buran* warships decided to make a run right through the middle of the squadron.

On the other hand, instead of the usual Type-3-Extended beams at the far ends on other corvettes, his little scout had two massive sensor arrays, giving him eyes comparable to one of the galactic survey cruisers. And a punch like a two-week-old kitten.

But if that was a freighter over there, they were completely unarmed. The AI overlord *Buran* didn't allow guns on any ship piloted solely by humans. Still, if he spotted *CS-405* somehow, the area would be flooded with angry warships in a couple of days, at most.

"Sensors," Phil said, after Brinich had a few moments to study everything. "What do we know?"

"As of an hour ago, they hadn't see us," he replied. "Or they assumed we were a rock, but if they could even see us from there, I'll eat their cargo myself. Ship's broadcasting navigational information on all channels, so I think we're safe. Plus, they haven't hopped over to inspect us."

"That's a civilian ship, Evan," Siobhan snarked lightly. "They have to program their JumpDrive manually after each step. Probably be here four or five hours just figuring out where they are, from what I read in the intelligence summaries."

"Passive sensors only," Phil interrupted before the two of them started another sibling-rivalry-session. They were professionals, but could get a little out of hand occasionally, like his own kids, Yi Wen and Yong Sheng. "And keep us running away. Last thing we need is to be sitting here when a Megalodon shows up."

Both nodded and subsided. They knew the score today. Undergunned, lost, and far from home.

"Phil," Siobhan said after a beat. "I was just forward talking to Julius Gephardt about food. Do we need to think about turning pirate?"

"How far can we go on current consumables?" he asked.

"About three weeks before it gets dicey," she replied. "That freighter should have a good supply of food. We might even get lucky and it's hauling something we can eat in the cargo bay."

"It's probably oatmeal," Evan turned and teased the Second Officer slyly.

Phil nearly fell out of his chair stifling a laugh, in spite of how dangerous the current situation was. Some crews got dark and quiet when things were like this. He had a crew of practical jokers and stand-up comedians.

Siobhan looked like she wanted to maybe kill and eat

Evan. She might, if oatmeal was the alternative. The whole crew knew her opinion on that topic.

"Engineering, Kosnett again," Phil pressed a comm button.

"Tuason, sir," the watch yeoman replied instantly.

"Ask Kam and Bok if they could get the emergency JumpSail working for a short flight," Phil ordered.

"How short, sir?"

"Fifty minutes RealSpace, Yeoman," Phil said. "And then be prepared to run like hell if we need to after that."

"Standby."

"Confirm a light freighter over there," Evan said into the silence. "Transponder's unencrypted, but the manifest just lists general cargo without telling us details. And he's going to need a full engine overhaul soon, looking at his output curve. Good enough to make it a couple more runs, but I'm guessing it's a private ship with razor-thin margins and he's pushing his hardware as hard as he dares."

"We all are, Evan," Phil said, waiting.

"Phil, this is Kam," the Chief Engineer came on the line. "Bok says he might be able to get you the first thirty seconds of flight, but we'll need several hours after that to start a rebuild. Is it worth it?"

Good question.

On the one hand, fresh intel on what *Buran's* folks knew, which was probably nothing, since this ship had been pointed towards *Severnaya Zemlya*. Most likely, they didn't know about the raid. Against that, there was the possibility of extra food, which was likely to be the first issue they ran into, going forward.

Downside, the risk of getting there just as that ship was ready to jump, and they got away, screaming about redcoats coming. The colonial militia wouldn't take long to return.

Phil considered that they could try to raid one of the

smaller colonies on the way home, but that same militia would have sent warning everywhere about the raid. And since Jessica had launched two big strikes, back to back, the locals would be skittish. And he only had a tiny crew.

"It's necessary," Phil decided. "I'll need one of your techs and a Damage Control team to go over with the Dragoon, Kam. We'll figure out after that if we need a prize crew or we just scuttle it. Hopefully, those folks are insured by *Buran* against the big, bad wolf."

# RESOLUTE REVOLUTION (DAY 95, COMMON ERA 13,449)

Lan was the better astrogator, so he normally calculated the jumps that took *Resolute Revolution* to the next port. However Kiel had asked him to cook dinner tonight, a task she usually handled, because she needed to perform some emergency maintenance on a worn generator.

*Resolute Revolution* was old. It had already proudly served two generations of merchants before Lan and Kiel were able to buy the vessel, nearly seven years ago now. Keeping the ship flying was frequently more an act of love for the old hardware than cold calculation of profit.

They could probably afford to sell this transport to the next generation of youngsters, just setting out, and buy themselves a new, or at least newer vessel. At forty-four years standard, and Kiel's forty-seven, they had talked. One more run to the sector capital and then home, and they probably would do just that.

They were not rich, not even wealthy, but they had done well enough for themselves, and provided the *Lord of Winter* with four, strong children. They could look forward to an era of not working themselves into exhaustion to make a profit. Perhaps even take the occasional vacation.

In the past, their only holidays had been to haul the by-chance, paying customer between stars, sharing tales of places they had been and sights they had seen.

Maybe they needed to buy a vessel that could haul several passengers, next time. Haul less cargo and more people, so they didn't get too lonely or withdrawn as they fast-approached the magical, middle-point of fifty years old. He made a mental note to ask Kiel her thoughts, after she finished cleaning up.

The kitchen was small, as befit an old vessel like *Resolute Revolution*. Just enough space for one person to work effectively, while the second stood across the small bar where the two of them normally ate their meals together.

Lan had just pulled a casserole from the oven when the proximity alarm sounded.

He stood there, bewildered for a moment, trying to make sense of the sound. The ship was not under thrust. And they were still at least two jumps away from the sector capital.

What in the world might be getting close to them? The scanners had shown nothing moving with any vector that threatened them.

Still, the alarm would continue to sound, growing progressively louder, until he clambered up to the bridge to disable it and dealt with whatever problem the old systems had identified. Probably a wiring fault, again.

And he was holding a casserole dish in one hand, still steaming with the last of the fresh vegetables from *Surgut*.

Lan wavered for a second longer, and then turned the stove off, opened the door, and slid the dish back in. It would remain warm enough, but hopefully not overcook.

He raced forward, climbing the stairs to the cockpit from which he could see to land.

Winded, he hurriedly checked the scan while he activated the pitiful power absorbers and prepared to turn the thrusters to full power. Lan assumed a dark rock he had missed on the first pass, one that had snuck up on him over the last two hours while he prepared dinner and Kiel fixed things.

The radio light was blinking.

He was being hailed?

By whom?

Lan activated the scanners and sent a ping outward.

His jaw dropped open as the signal appeared. Right on top of him, almost. Dead stop relative, but close enough to have set off the proximity alarms?

No, there was a smaller signal, coming closer. A shuttle?

The light blinked.

"Hello?" Lan said into it, still at a loss for what he was seeing on the screen.

"This is the *Imperial Fribourg Fleet*," a woman's voice announced gravely. "You will heave to and prepare to be boarded."

"What?"

"You are now a prisoner of war, Sri," the woman continued. "Surrender or you will be destroyed."

"What are you talking about?" Lan cried. "This is a civilian cargo ship."

On the screen, everything went bright white for a second as that other ship fired a single beam weapon. It missed, but not by much. And with neither of them moving, Lan understood the warning for what it is.

"Fine," Lan announced. "We surrender. The airlock is aft and port, just ahead of the bay doors. Try not to break anything. We were just sitting down to dinner."

"What's for dinner?" another woman's voice chimed in.

Lan was even more confused now. Dinner? Were these barbarians hungry, too? What was the universe coming to?

"Rockfish," Lan finally sputtered. "With vegetables in a cheese sauce with panko. Who are you people?"

"We're the *Fribourg Empire, Resolute Revolution*," the first woman growled. "The boarding party will join you shortly. Are there any crew besides the two of you?"

"What? No," Lan barked. "What's this all about?"

"We're taking you and your ship prisoner, Sri," she answered. "We will be boarding with guns shortly."

"Fine," Lan cut the line.

He stewed for a second before he opened the intercom, unsure where his spouse was at, right this moment.

"Kiel, dearest," he said. "Could you join me in the kitchen? I think we're having company for dinner."

# INVASION (APRIL 4, 402)

DRAGOON ON A SCOUT CORVETTE had not been Trinidad Mildon's dream, growing up. Not even in the top one hundred options. He had wanted to be an actor. Had studied the dramatic arts, both stage and music. Was all set to be a leading man, until he stopped growing at one hundred seventy-two centimeters. Short for a guy. Still a nickel taller than the Boatswain, but Bok was the only man in the crew Trinidad could say that about.

However, part of being an actor was training for action roles. Learning how to fight with hands and guns. Turned out he was way better at that part, although he could still cry on command.

Somehow, he had ended up teaching other actors how to do it. The shooting and punching bits. And gotten in with a group of retired navy folks doing the same thing. Listening to their stories of when they had been kids. One thing led to another.

Which was how he found himself at the airlock hatch to a *Buran* freighter, armored up in a combat suit with a pulse pistol in hand, surrounded by three of his people and a couple of others, about to technically invade a foreign country.

In the back of his mind, Trinidad found himself waiting for the director to yell *Action*.

"Boarding team, no change in status," Heather Lau said over the secured comm. "Two life signatures forward from you, same deck. Nothing else. Not even rats."

"Roger that, Tactical," Trinidad replied.

One last glance around to make sure everyone was ready, getting nods. Nakisha had a ram, in case they needed to shatter a door lock. Vlad and Gerry had pistols like him.

Time to get serious.

Trinidad reached up and turned on the spots on both sides of his helmet. *Lights*.

He checked the recording and transmission gear. *Camera*.

Trinidad keyed the external override on the airlock, once it agreed that the pressure inside had equalized. *Action*.

Muted beeping as the door opened outward into the shuttle's airlock. Trinidad had the pistol in his left hand, and his right hand, the blocker, free, just in case there was a fighting robot or something on the other side of the door. His job would be to stop it long enough for Nakisha to blow it to pieces with her pulse rifle.

Nothing.

Well, dingy. Just like one of those bad vids he had been an extra in, once upon a time. Not enough lighting. Walls that had been painted a long time ago, but were fading to rusty bland now.

He wondered if it would smell like mold, or fresh paint and newly-cut lumber, like a movie set, if he opened his faceplate to sniff the air. Maybe later. Gas attacks were always an option in defending tight corridors. That was why his team were in combat suits. Full life support, and reasonable armor against surprises.

Still, nothing.

Trinidad poked his head out and looked both ways. Central corridor, right down the spine, from his guess. The airlock was pretty deep, so all the cabins were probably the same depth and this one had just had an outer hatch added.

Aft, a closed hatch across the corridor that felt like the engine room. According to Evan Brinich, the cargo deck ran the whole length of the ship, just below this, with hatches at both ends to allow smooth loading and unloading. And it was currently several degrees below freezing down there.

He turned and stepped out of the airlock, facing forward. More dinginess. Place felt old. Not horror movie bad, just run down. Of course, he was used to a brand new ship, with a crew of people constantly cleaning and fixing things. Didn't look like much of that happened here.

"Hello?" he yelled, keying the external speakers.

"In here," a woman's voice yelled back, echoing down the corridor from somewhere forward.

This was nothing like training. Or a movie. In the action sequence, the good guys would be lined up down corridor, ducked into doorways, desperately trying to stop the bad guys from storming the ship and capturing the princess.

Grenades. Cross-fire. Smoke. Ominous music.

Something.

A glance back. Nakisha didn't help when she shrugged at him.

"I'll lead," he announced, mostly just to look like he was in charge.

There was a light on, from an open doorway to port, ten or twelve meters forward. It spilled out like moonlight against the dinginess. Audio pickups caught what sounded like metal utensils on plates. Had they been serious about eating dinner? While being boarded?

Trinidad scowled inside his helmet and squared his shoulders.

He edged forward, staying tight against the starboard wall, letting Nakisha stay to port and cover the long hallway against sudden surprises. Gerry and Ivan trundled along like crabs, watching backwards and staying back far enough that a grenade didn't get everyone.

Doorway.

Trinidad caught movement inside and brought up the pistol.

He found himself looking at the back of a man's head, bent over and slurping something from a spoon.

"Nobody move," Trinidad yelled in Mandarin.

*Great, now it sounds like a hold-up. I wish the writer was here to come up with better dialogue. Maybe we'll get lucky and this whole sequence will end up on the cutting room floor, or something.*

The man glanced back. Nobody was supposed to be that calm with a gun pointed at them. Not even in movies.

There was a woman as well. She leaned to one side to look across the bar at him.

"Hello," she replied in the same language. "Lan says you're pirates? What are you doing here?"

"Taking you into custody, ma'am," Trinidad answered, wishing he didn't feel like the villain. Still, it was a paycheck, even if there wouldn't be any residuals from this one.

"Can we finish dinner first?" the man asked.

Trinidad stepped to the doorway, but not inside. The room was small. Too tiny for fighting, if the man suddenly moved. Better to let the door frame contain him.

He looked Asian. That northern Asian look that Keller's ambassador had about him. Eyes with the extra fold, but still more round. Skin more golden-brown than one of the Chinese Diaspora. Black hair buzzed tight against his skull.

Average height, so a little taller than Trinidad, and built kinda squishy.

The woman was the same, except she was a little shorter than Trinidad, and her hair was a little longer than the man's. Otherwise, they might have been twins.

Trinidad reached up with his free hand and popped open his faceplate, shifting to local atmosphere for now. Damn, that smelled good. Some sort of meat in a cheese sauce, with vegetables in the mix.

"Go ahead," Trinidad decided.

This might be their last nice meal for a while. He had no idea what Commander Kosnett would do with the prisoners, but everyone back on *405* was gossiping about food right now. When it might run out. How the boss would react.

"Is there anybody else aboard?" he asked.

"Just my spouse and I," the man said, picking up a spork and digging back into the bowl before him.

Trinidad's gun had never wavered. Neither of them had so much as blinked.

Had they been so far behind lines that they forgot there was a war going on? Hell, this deep in enemy space, did their AI master even tell them that there were rebels against the galactic order, still fighting?

Trinidad really felt the need for some theme music right now.

"Nakisha, Gerry, check forward," Trinidad said. "Clear every room but don't touch anything."

A text message appeared on the Heads Up Display (HUD) on the right side of Trinidad's helmet. "*What's for dinner?*" it asked. Probably Siobhan. Evan had mentioned her and brought up oatmeal.

Trinidad stepped far enough into the room that he could manually zoom his camera on the dish in the middle of the bar, and then over to where the woman was eating.

"*Looks yummy*," the next line read.

Trinidad had to agree. Smelled fantastic, too. These people might fit in with Centurion Gephardt, if they cooked like that on a normal day.

The man turned and studied Trinidad now as he watched. The crewman shrugged.

"I would like to stow everything in the refrigerator now," he said. "Could you step back please? You're in front of the door."

Seriously, no scenario in his head had ever played out like this.

"I am Centurion Trinidad Mildon," he told them, trying to retain some level of control of the situation. On his local comm, he could hear Nakisha snickering, listening in. "Dragoon of *CS-405*. We'll be taking you into custody now."

"Well, watch the left-hand auxiliary generator, as you face it from the hatch," the woman said. "It's acting up again and I was halfway through checking the filters and resetting baselines. I guess you'll have to do that tomorrow."

Trinidad stopped himself before he actually shook his head in disbelief. He could hear Nakisha's laughter echoing down the corridor from the bow.

"Just come with me," he finally said in an exasperated sigh.

"Fine," the man said. "But you're doing dishes."

# SALVAGE (APRIL 5, 402)

KAM PULLED her head and shoulders back out of the opening and looked up at Phil and Bok, poised close by and obviously waiting on pins and needles. She found it funny that the casing to the captured ship's JumpDrive was too narrow for even Phil's shoulders, let alone Bok's, without taking the entire thing apart first.

"Well?" Phil asked.

"Seems to work just fine," she said with an elaborate shrug.

She reached down and picked up a small, confiscated engineering tablet and keyed the button to bring it live. It was a cheap model. Two dimensional touch screen, without even a projector.

Everything was in Mongolian, according to the words she had looked up, but Keller had made sure the whole squadron was prepared to read anything captured. And most of what Kam needed was graphical anyway. Legible enough for her needs.

Not many people in the squadron spoke the language yet, but there were numerous training and conversational videos that the Ambassador had recorded before he left, just in case.

"Good news, we can steal this ship and fly it somewhere," she continued, answering Phil's unasked question. "But there's nothing in here we could strip out in order to fix our primary JumpSail. The technology isn't even the same, although I can see where Henri Baudin started, back when he invented the new system."

Bok nodded. Phil cursed under his breath before turning to the Boatswain.

"Complete rewire of the secondaries?" he asked.

"Mostly done," the older man shrugged. "The control circuits we could sometimes replace from spares and parts salvaged from the primary, but it's a hack-job. Nowhere near as stable or safe as they did at the factory when they built it. We're going to have problems with heat build-up and power fluctuations all over the place. Not sure how quickly we'll burn out parts never intended for something like this, but I wouldn't want to go more than a few hours at a time in JumpSpace, at least until we know how well we can hold everything together."

"Did we learn anything from the prisoners?" Phil pressed.

Kam laughed.

"Old married couple, out seeing the galaxy as merchant traders," she said. "Almost remind me of my parents that way. Friendly enough, once they got over their shock. Ship's not all that impressive, but at least the cargo is something useful."

"Yes," Phil agreed. "Several thousand kilograms of frozen tuna steaks will go a long way towards keeping us in space, plus the little bit we can strip from Lan and Kiel's cupboards, if we decide not to keep the ship."

She watched him stand more fully and run through some internal dialogue, eyes focused on a far bulkhead for a moment.

"We need to keep our options open," he finally said. "Kam, Bok, split your teams however you need to. I want this ship tuned and cleaned up so we can trust using it, long term. Or so we can at least pay Kiel and Lan back for borrowing it, if we decide we've gotten all the use out of it we can and end up dropping them off somewhere. Then get the systems on *405* as fixed as you can. We need to get clear of this area as soon as humanly possible, and find a path home that doesn't run us right into more of these ships jumping around."

"Will do," she said, standing as Phil turned and headed forward.

She turned to find Bok almost as pensive as Phil had been.

"Thoughts?" she asked the Boatswain.

"Want to get some of my people over here," he said. "We'll need a damage control party flying on this boat, with whoever you assign. They'll need to work directly with you, training, while I take a team and get our ship to the point where we can move."

"Sounds like a plan," Kam said. "Send over Jules when you get back. I need him to decide how to move the cargo. Looks like we can keep some of it here, but I'd like to shift a bulk over to fill freezers forward. What can we do, if we run out of space?"

"Throw it all inside a couple of insulated barriers and tack it to the outside of the hull?" Bok suggested. "Can't imagine Phil's going anywhere near a star for a while, so deep space cold will be just as good."

"Throw Dunklin on that," she ordered. "We'll use his redneck skills to dream something up."

"On it, boss," Bok nodded and departed.

Kam took a deep breath and looked back down at ten-thousand-year-old technology nobody on their side even understood anymore. She was pretty sure she could fix this. Probably fix it all, with access to the original design specifications and a competent engineering shop.

What the hell was Phil going to do with a broken-down freighter?

# PRIZE (APRIL 5, 402)

"Good news first," Phil found himself saying as he and Siobhan looked at each other across the bridge's day office table. "There will be no oatmeal in your foreseeable future."

"But?" she asked, waiting for the other shoe to land.

"Lots of fish," Phil grinned. "I want you to take command of the other ship as part of a prize crew."

"What about Heather?" the woman asked carefully. "Shouldn't she be your first pick?"

"Heather's already set to get her own command, as soon as one opens," Phil confided. "First Lord knows better than to offer her a destroyer on a quiet frontier, so I expect there will be orders waiting for her, once we get back to civilization. She'll likely head home and pick up a new corvette coming off the line, get herself a crew trained up, and come back here to help us. Time for you to exercise an independent command."

Siobhan was always hard to read. The woman kept her feelings and ideas close to the vest, except for oatmeal. Right now, he got to watch her go through something like the entire stages of death in a heartbeat: shock, elation, concern, and distrust.

"What's the catch?" she finally asked.

"You're going to be largely on your own for most things," Phil told her. "Once you figure out how to navigate and fly the old beast, you'll have to scout ahead of us while we limp to someplace where we can steal more food. If you get into trouble, there will be almost nothing we can do to help you."

"We're on our own now, Phil," she observed dryly.

"Yes, but you'll be exercising command authority, Siobhan," he replied. "I'll have to share certain things with you that only Heather has known, up until now. And you'll be subject to Keller's Order 48."

"Oh, shit," Siobhan said quietly.

"Exactly, Siobhan," Phil commiserated.

Jessica Keller was a brilliant commander. Possibly one of the best *Aquitaine* ever produced. She was also a cold, vicious bitch when it came to her personal war with *Buran* on behalf of *Fribourg* and Centurion Wiegand. Thus: Order 48, only the most notorious of her standing command orders for this fleet.

*No commanding officer, including Tactical Officers who exercise command authority in combat, can allow themselves to be taken prisoner by* Buran's *forces. They will exercise any and all options to evade capture, including self-termination, if the officer feels that is the only way to keep the information in his or her head out of enemy hands, in the event of probable torture.*

He watched Siobhan take a deep breath. Everyone knew about Order 48, but for most of the crews, it was only a theoretical thing. Only he and Heather had been required to sign that acknowledgement.

Up until now.

"Under my authority, we will impress the ship known as *Resolute Revolution* into *Aquitaine* service, Siobhan," he continued. "You will take command, subject to the normal rules and regulations of a brevet to command centurion. As the freighter is unarmed, you will serve as your own tactical officer, should it become necessary. Will you accept this commission?"

He waited, watching the sudden weight settle on her shoulders. She was within her rights to refuse, right now, with no black mark accruing on her record as a result. Other than losing his eventual recommendation for her own, independent command at a later date.

Not a career-killer, but…

"You said scouting, Phil?" she suddenly said carefully. "How far out were you thinking?"

"We're going to be hopping in and out of JumpSpace probably at least as much as you would be, Siobhan," he replied, trying to figure out the angle she was pursuing right now. "I'll need a clean path at first, and then we'll most likely need to raid someplace to get more food and intelligence. Keller will have this whole frontier lit up by now, so we'll have to sneak every step of the way. What are you thinking?"

She still hadn't said yes. Or no.

"Raiding," she replied with a hard glimmer in her eyes. "That ship isn't known as a pirate, right now. That's good for at least one surprise attack, somewhere. After that, it depends on the flow of information."

"Indeed it does, Centurion," Phil agreed, letting some level of formality creep into his voice. "High risk, commensurate reward."

"Can I pick my prize crew?" she finally asked the question he had been waiting for.

"Within certain vetoes, Siobhan," he said. "You can't have Kam, Bok, or Evan."

"Don't want them, Phil," she hesitated. "I want Trinidad, Nakisha Onks, Markus Dunklin, and Max Bathurst. That gives me a redneck engineer, a medic, and a couple of gunmen."

"We can probably swing that," he said. "What are you up to?"

"Building a wooden horse, Phil."

# MISSION LOG (APRIL 7, 402)

"Personal log: Command Centurion Phil Kosnett, commanding *RAN CS-405*. Current location: Deep in enemy space near *Severnaya Zemlya* with a broken scout, a stolen freighter, two prisoners, and a timer running on food.

Capturing *Resolute Revolution* has added more than two weeks to our available deadline before we end up breaking out the emergency rations, but it will still not get us home. As it now appears, we will need to top up on air and water first, as things will start getting thin in that time."

*Phil paused to take a breath, looking for the words he needed. Nobody was likely to listen to this log, unless he was dead, or made it home and the Court Martial he faced went especially bad. Nothing like speaking to the galleries and history.*

"I have tasked Centurion Skokomish with taking command of the freighter and becoming our own scout, assigning her a team that has all the makings of a modern pirate crew. It is my current belief that we simply cannot make a straight run home to our previous operating base, as Keller would take our disappearance as a risk that *CS-405* has been captured, and so must immediately move Forward Base

Omicron to a safer location. Thus, we will eventually need to cross the Gulf and make it through *Buran* patrols to reach safe harbor at an Imperial world.

With few habitable stars in the Gulf itself, we will have to raid at least one enemy system before undertaking the long sail across the darkness, both for intelligence and consumables. *CS-405* is one of the better ship classes to undertake such a mission, and I have high confidence that we can make it.

Repairs have the secondary JumpSail in some level of working order, but the primary will need to be pulled at a dry-dock and replaced *in toto*. Boatswain Bok Battenhouse has a file containing notes and suggestions for an improvement to the engineering design, to prevent a repeat.

His current theory is that the final shot that struck us, a hit on an aft panel partly tempered by the edge of a shield wall, triggered some sort of power spike in the generator, which burned out some of the control circuits. When we transitioned to JumpSpace, the generator began to overload, unable to properly regulate the power demands of the JumpSail itself, and created a feedback loop that eventually caused the system to fail explosively, taking out both JumpSail controllers."

*Phil paused again, contemplating the next steps. This was just about a worst nightmare for a command centurion, a wounded deer being stalked by tigers in the heavy brush.*

"Crew morale is good, at present. Food and consumables are plentiful enough at this time. The greatest risk will be raiding a system. Smaller planets typically have a small, automated station in orbit, which could provide us air and water, but we will still need to acquire food and intelligence. To do that, we will have to take it, either from another freighter such as *Resolute Revolution*, or capture it from a planet.

We can assault a station, or land the prize vessel on a surface, and conduct operations. The risk at that point is aggressive patrolling by *Buran*'s border fleet, in light of Keller's massive raids all along this border. We cannot face any enemy warship on even terms, as even a Hammerhead has us massively outgunned. Flight would be our only option in the occurrence, with any deployed crew potentially captured. Heather Lau and I will not leave *CS-405*, but Siobhan Skokomish will be aboard *Resolute Revolution*. She has acknowledged Rule 48 and signed the documents into ship's memory.

Hopefully, it will never come to that."

# QUEEN ANNE'S REVENGE (APRIL 7, 402)

SIOBHAN WAS in the starboard of the two seats up front, enjoying the vista of outer space through a big window, rather than her normal view on a screen. The seats swiveled inward on posts when you unlocked them to move, so she could turn around and talk without standing up. They weren't all that comfortable, but Lan and Kiel had kept them clean. Hell, the whole ship was clean, except for the kitchen, where Trinidad had assigned himself the task of handling all the leftover dishes.

Flying this ship, she had learned, pretty much involved a couple of flat-panel screens with programmable buttons on all four sides. You called up a function menu, and commands pointed at the associated button you needed to push. Primitive, but pretty much invulnerable to time and wear.

A sound behind her caused Siobhan to turn.

"Сайн байна уу," Siobhan said with a grin as Trinidad stepped onto the cramped bridge.

"What the hell was that?" Trinidad replied, stopped dead by the gibberish coming out of her mouth.

"Mongolian," Siobhan said. "I said hello. As of right now,

this whole vessel is going to be conversational Mongolian, whenever possible. You've got the videos from the Ambassador and Bhattacharya to watch. Plus all the stuff I downloaded. I don't care how good your Mandarin is. The places we're going won't necessarily speak it, and I figure we'll need to do some really fast talking."

Trinidad nodded.

"You and Nakisha are probably the best at that, then," he said after a moment. "I can see what I'll be doing after dinner. Until then, what's the plan? Phil said something about a Trojan horse?"

"There is not enough food to get everyone home," Siobhan replied. "Chances of us finding another ship like this are low, so we have to go take it from someone. To do that, we have to walk right up to them, all casual like, before we pull out guns."

"And *Resolute Revolution*?" he pressed.

"We have to become someone else," she grinned. "Did some research and found us an awesome ship name, but Heather vetoed it. At least until I dug out the thesaurus and made it less obvious. Got Markus aft, changing the IFF transponder now."

"What name did Heather say no to?" he asked.

"*Queen Anne's Revenge*," Siobhan replied. "It was a famous pirate ship, way back into the pre-starflight days. Maritime pirates. Sailing on water."

"Huh," Trinidad grunted something that sounded to her more like a placeholder than anything. "Okay, so who are we now?"

"*Anna's Vindication*," she laughed. "Close enough, and not like anybody is ever going to get the joke."

"So what happened to the original?" he pressed. "*Queen Anne's Revenge*?"

"According to the files I read, she was grounded off the

coast of the country of North America in the early Eighteenth Century, pre-Starflight Era," Siobhan said. "The command centurion offloaded his crew to other ships, and as much treasure as they could, before splitting up. The guy was named Blackbeard, and whole legendary mythologies still abound about him."

"So he got away?" Trinidad asked. "I thought that pirates always got caught, eventually."

"Well, the system said he accepted a pardon from a colonial governor, not long after the ship was sunk," she explained. "But then went back to being a pirate within a year. Eventually, the authorities caught up with him and killed him. Couple of centuries later, they found the ship, and excavated it. Sometime after that, some crazy, rich guy built a full replica and sailed it around for the longest time before it ended up in a museum. But, yeah, most of the pirates I looked up all got taken down eventually. That's why I chose *Anna's Vindication*. She got away."

Siobhan nearly laughed when Trinidad reached out a hand and rapped on a bulkhead lightly with one fist. Every spacer she knew was superstitious enough to touch a hull like that for luck.

"Works for me," he said quietly.

"So you came up here for something before I sidetracked you," Siobhan remembered.

"Right," he snapped his fingers. "Everything is finally stowed aft. You're in Lan and Kiel's cabin. The rest of us are hanging hammocks in other places for now. We're ready as soon as you are."

"Sounds good," she said. "Let everyone know they should get ready to depart. I'll call Phil, and as soon as they say go, we're jumping somewhere so we can figure out what it feels like and how hard it will be to navigate."

"And we're off," he said, turning and bouncing down the eight steps.

Siobhan watched him go. For everyone else, their job was easy. Trinidad and Nakisha hopefully only had to point guns at people, and not actually shoot anyone. Max was along in case someone got hurt. Markus was mostly good, with the cut on his arm healing well, and was the best redneck engineer she knew. He would keep them flying and breathing.

She had the hard part: playing the role of Edward Teach, the infamous Blackbeard.

Maybe the most fun part, as well.

Hopefully, she wouldn't end up like he had.

"*CS-405*, this is the prize," Siobhan began, opening the comm relay. At no point was she going to use names, even encrypted and on a laser. Who knew what magic a *Sentient* starship could weave to decipher it all?

"Go ahead," Heather came on the line a moment later.

"We are all stowed here, Heather," Siobhan said. "Initial target has been identified on our nav charts and we're ready for our first jump. Conservative estimate seventy to eighty hours to reach our rendezvous."

"Acknowledged, prize," Heather replied. "Initiate when ready. We're right behind you."

"See you on the far side," Siobhan closed the line. Hopefully, the far side wasn't death, and everyone would be waiting for them when they arrived.

"All hands, this is your commander," she said, switching to the interior announcement system. "Stand by for transition."

Siobhan took a deep breath and considered the third button along the top of the screen in front of her. She had done all the math, reviewed the engineering logs, and read about all the places Lan and Kiel had gone to, at least what little she had been able to find in *405*'s systems. The rest awaited her taking the time to translate the ship's logs more cleanly. Another task for later.

Now she had to throw herself into the darkness, trusting a Jump system she had never imagined she would ever have to use.

Ten thousand years of successful navigation, she reminded herself. We escaped the mother solar system and colonized the galaxy with that technology.

*Here goes nothing.*

Siobhan pressed the button. Around her, *Anna's Vindication* seemed to shimmer once, and then they were gone.

# THE LONG RUN (APRIL 7, 402)

"Engineering, this is the bridge," Phil said in a firm, authoritative voice. He knew this tape would be played at his next Court Martial, regardless of outcome. Might as well make it sound good for the Fleet Centurions who would be sitting in judgment that day.

"Rushforth here," Kam replied a beat later.

"Stand by for powered flight," he announced. "Pilot, take us out."

"Acknowledged," both Kam and West Lovisone managed at the same moment.

West was flying, for now. Normally, Evan would have shifted responsibilities, but Phil needed the man on the sensors.

There was no sudden wiggle of acceleration as the engines began to push the solid mass of *CS-405*, so the gravplates were still stable everywhere. Nothing in the world like losing internal systems integrity when maneuvering. No, just a little distance indicator number slowly getting larger, since it was locked on *Severnaya Zemlya.*

And they were finally, successfully, running away.

On Phil's personal screen, the way forward was clear. Emptiness beckoned, like a hidden siren luring sailors onto the rocks. He almost felt like Moses, standing on a suddenly-dry shore, with all of *Pharaoh Buran*'s armies closing in behind him.

"Ship underway," West announced, looking up with a serious face that still seemed to be all smiles. "Acceleration constant. All systems within tolerances."

It wasn't often the Yeoman got a chance to shine. Siobhan had been so good at her job that Phil had let her monopolize things, perhaps a little too much. But she had the makings of a good command centurion, one of these days, and it was one of his jobs to see that she could get there. Now it was West's turn.

Phil nodded back and waited. Kam's face was a small image on the left side of his personal screen, looking away and talking silently to someone close by aft, with the line muted.

*Queen Anne's Revenge* was already gone. Phil had heard the whole story from Heather, and agreed with the rename, but in his mind, the original name would probably stick forever. *Anna's Vindication* sounded so much less impressive. Less martial.

Pretty good for a wolf in sheep's clothing, though.

He looked down again and found her face on the screen.

"Kam, everything still stable?"

Her eyes came back to the screen and found his, then flickered away to take in all the readouts she had in front of her. His was boiled down to just a few, but hers always looked like a musician's mixing board: virtual sliders, knobs, and gauges ranging over any possible thing the engineers need to tweak electronically. Plus a few that could only be torqued with a two-meter prybar.

"Everything's green so far, bridge," Kam finally said.

Phil nodded and switched to the public address system.

"All hands, stand by for transition to JumpSpace," he said.

More fodder for Court Martial. Unlike many places, and much of human history, the *Republic of Aquitaine* Navy used frequent, public Courts to render judgment after the fact. Not just to punish, but to make it clear that a command centurion in a bad situation had made the best possible choice among bad ones.

They considered it a training tool, and Phil agreed. The interesting decision sequences were frequently taught at the Academy, straight out of the Court's records, so new officers coming up would understand how bad things could get, and see which choices would be acceptable. And which might get you cashiered.

Right now, Phil figured he was slightly better than fifty/fifty to lose his command when he got home. Much of it would depend on what the engineers found when they pulled apart the ass-end of his ship, something he really couldn't do until they were all safely home.

If the design itself had flaws, then much of the blame would fall elsewhere. If not, then he had held the responsibility to train his officers better, and had failed. He didn't think that was possible, with Kam and Bok, but anything could happen, especially in the light of retrospective expertise.

For now, he needed to make sure that the rest of his crew followed clear orders, so that everything else would fall on his head, if it had to roll over this. That their careers wouldn't be ended if his was.

Command Centurion in the *RAN* was a heavy responsibility, even in a tiny, largely-unarmed scout corvette. But this was war, and they were all warriors. He had to get his people home. And then, if he could, exact as much damage to *Buran's* war-fighting capabilities as he could.

"Pilot, make your jump," Phil finally ordered, allowing what he thought was the right amount of time for everything to build up and weigh on people.

This would hopefully work.

The transition was *weird*. Phil had no other word to describe it. Some people had described the normal transition as falling suddenly into a pool of warm mud, causing you to float in happy medium. Coming out was just the opposite: warm and damp becoming suddenly dry.

This had a sharp flex to it. Not painful, like a punch to the gut, but a giant hand grabbing you from behind and briefly squeezing your entire ribcage, just the least amount. The air had the lightest tang, like someone had just opened a lemonade mix and let too much powder poof up into the air.

Maybe he was imagining it. It was gone almost as fast as it had occurred.

Except West had the strangest look on his face, as did Evan.

Henri Baudin had invented the modern JumpSail, right before he went on to *Found* the nation of *Aquitaine*. The secondary unit they had just engaged was a design that probably was finalized in his lifetime and then left alone. Phil had never been on a ship that used one before.

That would change, if he ever got home. Everyone would have to use the secondary from time to time, just to prove it was working. And maybe tasted like lemons.

"Status?" Phil called out.

This was the iffy part. They had rebuilt the emergency Sail's controllers, but there was only so much testing you could do. At least this first hop was intended to be short. Just an hour in JumpSpace at most, if everything held, and then drop back out and recalibrate everything.

Assuming nothing important melted in the meantime.

"Running hot but stable, sir," West called.

"Kam?" he followed up.

"Concur, Phil," she said, looking away and talking out of the corner of her mouth. "Putting Bok and his team on it. I'll scram the drive from here if we need to."

Phil realized he had been holding his breath. He let it go slowly, silently. Nobody needed to know how tight he was right now. They needed a calm example of unruffled leadership in front of them.

A commander infects his crew. If he panicked, they would join him quickly. If they panicked, then he must become the rock upon which such dread will founder.

"Very good," Phil announced. "Evan, I'll be in the office doing paperwork. You have the bridge for now. Heather, go off duty and get some sleep."

The last comment was addressed over the internal comm. Emergency Bridge was almost always listening in, so they could step up in a pinch, a virtual extension of the room here.

*CS-405* had just made the first step in what would be a very long run home.

# PRISONERS OF WAR (DAY 98?, COMMON ERA 13,449)

LAN EVENTUALLY FOUND the new circumstances interesting, once he got over his rage at being kidnapped by barbarians. And having his ship stolen.

The nerve of these people.

Still, he and Kiel had been kept together, unharmed, in a cabin larger than the one they had previously shared aboard *Resolute Revolution*. The walls were a soothing foam green color, with the floor painted a brown probably intended to evoke wood. The bed had proven to be extremely comfortable, and they had been fed regularly by a group of armed men and women who were singularly uncommunicative.

At least the room had a video presentation system, even if most of the choices were unintelligible. Few of the movies or entertainment shows were even in Mandarin, and none had Mongolian sub-titles.

The only reason he hadn't gone insane was that at the first meal, the gunmen had brought a pair of fancy tablet computers loaded to the top with books. Interestingly, many were originally published by the *Lord of Winter*, rather than the barbarians, so Lan assumed they had been looted at some point.

At least he had enough material to keep his mind engaged for perhaps as long as a year. Kiel read faster than he did, so she would probably emerge in one hundred and eighty-two days needing new material.

Right now, she was on the bed, reading. Lan had found that the tablet also contained a text input system, so he was recording his observations and memories of the last few days. It helped him get over his pique.

These people had been polite, but they were still barbarians.

The door opening suddenly caused both he and Kiel to look up in surprise. Lunch (had it been lunch?) had been served only a few hours ago. Certainly, it was too early for whatever the next meal should be?

A woman in partial armor, face-shielded-helmet, and short rifle entered, standing impassively to one side. She wasn't threatening anyone, at least not any more than her mere presence was a threat.

Lan felt his simmering rage bubble, just a bit, so perhaps it was good that obvious and overwhelming violence was available on their part. Kiel would certainly counsel caution, but she was like that. It was one of the reasons he had been so happy when she chose him. Kiel completed him in ways he had not understood as a younger man.

Another soldier entered. This one had a pistol, but it was holstered. It took Lan a moment to realize the new visitor was also a woman. She was tall and wearing the same partial armor as the first, but she lacked a helmet, with red hair shorn almost as short as Kiel kept her darker locks.

The face said European, with rounded cheek bones and pale, almost bleached out skin, compared to he or Kiel. Her eyes were an interesting blue, so rare in *The Holding*, but apparently common among the barbarians. He had just never met one before the group that stole their freighter.

"Commander ask talk you," she said in a slow, laborious voice, obviously trying to work her way through a new language.

It was interesting that she tried Mongolian, when the barbarians already knew that he and Kiel were fluent in Mandarin. But that was also a barbarian tongue.

Perhaps there was hope for these savages.

With a careful eye on the armed soldier, Lan set down his tablet and looked over at Kiel. She nodded and did the same. While she slid over to the edge of the bed, Lan rose slowly. Non-threateningly.

As a typical male of *The Protectorate of Man*, Lan was taller than Kiel, and heavier. Stronger overall, but probably not as tough. Either of these foreign women looked like they could handle him without assistance. The way they both stood conveyed that utter conviction that they were safe here. Being on an alien (enemy?) starship meant that he had nowhere to go, even if he was stupid enough to start something.

Plus, they had asked, rather than marching in and ordering him about. Perhaps there *was* hope for these people.

"Yes," Lan said simply.

He stepped close to Kiel and took her hand. It was a promise far older than these newcomers. He drew much of his strength from his spouse.

"You come?" the redhead said carefully, her accent rendering the words almost impossible, but her body language conveying the rest fairly accurately.

She stepped back, into the corridor and to the right. The other soldier stepped away from the door as he and Lan approached it, and then followed them.

"We will follow you," Kiel said slowly.

It took Lan a moment, and then he realized she was enunciating the words in such a way that the other woman would learn. Perhaps there would be language lessons soon. Kiel had always been better at picking up new terms and new languages.

He wondered what the barbarians spoke at home.

The hallway was just as impressive as the cabin had been. Large and airy. Lacking any oil or rust stains anywhere, or perhaps cleaned up. The hallway was nearly three meters across, where *Resolute Revolution*'s main corridor was barely more than a meter.

Nobody would have to turn sideways as their partner needed to get by, and use it as a cheap excuse to grope their spouse when she did.

Lan felt Kiel squeeze his hand. He glanced over at her and realized, from the grin on her face, that she had probably reached the same conclusion. Briefly, he felt sorry for the barbarians, to miss something like that, but he also remembered that this was a warship, with a crew of perhaps hundreds, and not an old married couple who might occasionally stop and snuggle in the hallway, because they could. Lan squeezed her hand back.

*Warship.*

He had heard rumors that the barbarians had armed ships without aspects of *The Eldest* in charge. He wondered what it must be like to live without proper guidance. To flail aimlessly about, lacking the subtle wisdom and memories of a God to give your life structure and order.

But that was why they were barbarians, after all. They had not seen the wisdom of joining *The Holding* voluntarily. Had resisted, as pitifully as that might be, while *The Eldest* continued his course to eventually enroll all of lost humanity into the great project.

The *Lord of Winter* would help these barbarians come to their senses.

The tall redhead led them to another chamber, up a deck and some distance from their original cabin. The halls had remained remarkably empty, but Lan supposed that prisoners being moved about should be kept from the crew, so as not to endanger them.

As if a forty-four-year-old merchant with the slightest pot belly was a threat to body-builders with guns.

"Commander Officer here," the redhead said and gestured as the door opened.

The new room was larger than their cabin. A large, wooden table dominated it, with chairs all the way around. Two more soldiers with pistols stood watch on the far wall with faceplates down. In their armor, it was hard to gender them, especially considering how tall the woman escort was.

Not that it mattered, the commander was seated beyond the small sea of wood.

He rose as they entered, and smiled welcomingly. He was a big man as well, perhaps one hundred-eighty-eight centimeters tall. Broad in the shoulders and impressive, Lan guessed ninety-five kilograms, with muscles everywhere and dark, blond hair. Another European genotype, so common among the barbarians.

He gestured to the two chairs on this side of the table.

"Thank you for joining me," he began in Mandarin. "I understand you are fluent enough that we can converse?"

"We are," Kiel spoke up, moving to grab a chair and slide it back.

Interestingly, the legs of the chairs had magnets attached, holding to the floor, but allowing one to move it around easily enough. *Resolute Revolution's* chairs were either flip-down jumpseats that retracted to the hull when not in use, or sat on swivel posts, like the bridge.

Lan waited for his spouse to sit, and then joined her.

"Command Centurion Phil Kosnett," the tall, strange, pirate captain introduced himself. "Commander of this vessel, *CS-405*. My apologies that we had to commandeer your ship for the time being."

"The time being?" Kiel asked.

Lan knew his spouse was smarter than he was, so he let her talk to the barbarians now. Perhaps he could learn something, just watching.

"Yes," Kosnett said.

Kosnett. What a strange culture, to not have one of the eight Clan names, nor a crèche. Just a family group and a personal name. How bereft they must be, not to *belong*.

"I am Nu Ulap Narah Kiel," she introduced herself. "Half owner of the freighter *Resolute Revolution*. My spouse, Xi Arakh Goran Lan. How long are we to be prisoners, Command Centurion?"

They had not spoken previously with any of the officers in charge of this crew, just men and women with guns, however polite those people had attempted to be.

The man Kosnett had an expressive face. It was not an evil one, like that ethnotype frequently was in movies. Perhaps more the *Magic Anglo*.

"I would like to offer you a choice, Kiel," he said succinctly.

Lan was reminded of the ancient choice Faust made, when confronted by Mephistopheles. He wondered what black magics these foreign devils might have brought with them.

"Go on," Kiel replied coolly. She was always better at keeping her emotions in check than Lan found himself to be. She was the one who negotiated deals with new brokers, when they traveled to different planets.

Kosnett nodded and checked both of their faces before proceeding.

"Our ship suffered damage during a recent attack on *Severnaya Zemlya*," he said.

"You attacked the sector capital?" Kiel sounded as shocked as Lan felt.

"We were part of Jessica Keller's fleet," he admitted. "She did serious damage to the station before departing. This ship was unable to keep up, and has been left behind. This is a military secret, but there is nobody that you can tell it to currently. At some future point, it will not matter. We captured your ship of necessity, and will use it."

"And the choice you would offer us in blood?" Kiel sneered awesomely at the barbarian.

"Not blood," Kosnett corrected. "We are in the process of sneaking to a safe place, using your ship as a scout. I can deposit you at the first *Holding* planet we encounter, where you will be safe. Or you can choose to stay with us until we are safely home, at which time I will return your ship to you and send you on your way, hopefully with a new cargo to replace the one I have stolen from you. The risk in the interim is that you would be destroyed if we were."

Lan was shocked. Disbelief rose up and clouded his eyes, but Kiel reached out a hand and squeezed his, reminding him who he was. Deals with devils were never beneficial. Briefly, he wondered if *The Eldest* would punish them for not resisting more forcefully. As if there was anything they could have done.

And would it be better to escape with what they knew at the first opportunity, or get their ship back, if the man kept his spurious promise?

Carrots, dangled in front of cart horses.

"Just like that?" Kiel asked skeptically.

"Yes," the man agreed. "We are strangers here, and you

have been accidentally swept up in our larger web. If we were savages, it would have been easier to have simply killed you when we took your ship. That's not my way. Keller's war is with *The Eldest*, and civilians will be hurt. Have been hurt. But it was always contained violence. Once her point was made, at places like *Yenisei* and *Stanovoy*, she allowed people to escape her wrath, even if they floated right beneath us in orbit, unable to maneuver from the damage we had done to them while battle raged. She has also ordered us to behave as civilized folk in the houses of strangers."

Lan caught Kiel's nearly-silent gasp of shock. Felt it himself. That was a line straight from a training crèche video: behaving as civilized folk in the houses of strangers.

Kosnett could not have stumbled onto the phrase accidentally. The look on his face made that clear. No, he had spoken with a scholar of *The Holding* at some point. That much was obvious. Learned enough of their ways to conduct himself appropriately.

"And if we choose to remain?" Kiel asked. "To travel with you to whatever safe destination you might find? You would return our ship?"

"If I can," the man said. "This is war, and things happen. If I cannot, then I will find a way to make you whole."

It was another interesting turn of phrase. Lan wondered if the man understood that in the legal sense, as those words had a special meaning in *The Holding*. Losing *Resolute Revolution* would not cause them to fall into poverty. They had enough credit with *The Eldest* to start over, perhaps buying another old freighter and returning to their merchant ways.

To be *made whole* would possibly involve the barbarians giving them a new ship, if the old one was lost.

Kiel glanced over for his opinion. Lan nodded. He was pretty sure what her choice would be, but he would back her one hundred percent, either way. He would be nothing without this woman by his side.

"We will accompany you, then, Command Centurion Kosnett," she announced. "We will see your ways, that we can report them home when we return."

Lan wondered what *The Eldest* would say, if they came home in a barbarian ship, loaded with barbarian goods for trade. But was not the purpose of *The Holding* to bring the barbarians to civilization?

Internally, he chuckled that the fates had chosen two such unlikely messiahs to convey that message.

# PEEKING (APRIL 11, 402)

THE BRIDGE of *Anna's Vindication* was crowded, but Siobhan wanted everyone up here to see what she was seeing, as well as to understand what sneakiness she had in mind. She had the right-hand seat, looking out through the big, front windshield. Max was in the left seat, with Markus right behind him. Nakisha and Trinidad were crammed into the open hatch. They had arrived at this system ahead of *CS-405*, but that was partly due to Siobhan pushing her piloting.

There was a feel to JumpSpace. Every gravity well and hydrogen cloud you encountered altered your trajectory in unpredictable ways. With modern JumpSails, you just ended up doing something like the equivalent of tacking occasionally, or perhaps lagging over or under big systems you needed to get by. *Anna's Vindication* was using the older JumpDrives, so on top of it all, she could only throw herself on a certain vector blindly and hope she didn't miss her target zone by too much. Capable grav-sensors would have made this so much easier.

But Siobhan had discovered in herself something of a feel for it, after the second or third try. It was like trying to nail a deer with an arrow in a crosswind, while it was bounding back and forth away from you. She couldn't describe it, but when everything lined up just right, her fourth jump had been almost exactly on the bullseye, missing zero by less than three light seconds, over a distance of more than three light-years.

And, according to the old logs, the best Lan would have been able to do with a run like this was take nine hops, when she had done it in six, and just under half the time he would have.

"Where are we, anyway?" Max asked. "I was busy converting a closet to a medbay when you explained it over the PA earlier, and was mostly ignoring you."

Siobhan grinned at that. Max always had his priorities lined up right, and part of that was him assuming she knew what the hell she was doing. And she might even, at that.

"That's *Barnaul*," Nakisha spoke up before Siobhan could answer, pointing to the map Siobhan was displaying on her screen, scaled up for everyone to see. "A pimple on the ass-end of beyond. *Here there be dragons* kind of place."

"She right?" Max turned to face his new commander.

"More or less," Siobhan agreed. "It's a relatively new mining colony. Only about forty years old, according to Lan's notes. They were planning on heading out here on a jaunt sometime, bringing exotic foodstuffs from either *Severnaya Zemlya* or *Ninagirsu*. Maybe *Altai* itself, although the planet that gave this sector its name is a forgotten backwater these days."

"Okay, I'm missing something," Max said ruefully. He was good at that. "Why do we want to go there if Kiel and Lan were looking to haul them food? Wouldn't we want to hit a farming world?"

"The key word is exotics, Max," Siobhan said. "Think all those tuna steaks we have in back, only even weirder.

Kiel's notes say things like sides of cetacean or shark carcasses from *Rivers*. Or strange fruits from some of the more exotic worlds. Stuff like dreamberries or their cousins, the swampberries, that come from *Altai*. Those were originally bred up from a gooseberry bush, back in the *Concord* days, according to the encyclopedia that *405* translated for me."

"I get the feeling you had this in mind two minutes after Phil offered you command," Trinidad grinned at her.

"Two minutes before," she admitted with a laugh. "*How I would become a pirate, given the chance?*"

"Berries?" Max asked, still lost.

"Kiel has extensive notes on every inhabited system in the sector, and what sorts of trade goods might work well," Siobhan said. "She and Lan were really successful at what they did, right up until we stole their ship. All that tuna would have made them a nice profit, back at the capital."

"Okay, so what's the play?" Max pressed on.

Medics were always trying to get ahead of you, so they knew how to arrange a field hospital, based on expected injuries. If it was a party, then lots of aspirin, ice packs, and the staple gun. EVA assaults necessitated treatment for death-pressure exposure. Gun fights would mean salve and cotton bandages for pulse rifle burns or broken bones.

"So *Barnaul's* entire economy can be found in one, big, pit mine," Siobhan answered. "With a small landing field well off to one side, and a single, small town located just about between them. Map of the town is in the navigation system. Miners are mostly housed in barracks right at the top of the hole, well outside town, 'cause a shift goes down every eight hours to keep things humming, and only come into town on scattered rest days. The rest of the place is pretty quiet, and pretty provincial."

Siobhan paused long enough to swap the planetary view

for the map of the city. Two warehouses got highlighted in pink against the gray of the rest.

"So, we land about here," she said, adding a starburst to the map, clear up in what looked like a forgotten corner of the landing field, the northeast, when the road to town was in the southeast. "Note that we're accidentally almost right on top of the control tower for the field."

A circle turned crimson as she pressed a button.

"We land, as close to the middle of the night as possible," she continued. "Sneak out and capture the tower. Then we try to steal a truck or something, drive it to one of those two warehouses, and break in. The smaller one is mostly refrigerated or frozen goods. The big one has some food, and bunch of general supplies. It being the most efficient method, thought up by a most-efficient robot, everything for the colony is pretty much in one of those two places, with most stores only keeping a few days' worth of stuff on hand."

"Thank the Creator we stole this ship," Trinidad offered like a benediction. "Can you imagine trying something like this without good intel? Land blind and stumble our way around?"

"Oh, we're still going to do that, *Tee*," Siobhan replied. "You got what, six marines under your command?"

"That's right," he said.

"So my plan is to meet up with Phil and Heather," Siobhan continued. "Get all of your people, plus Bok and a couple of his teams for strong backs and bring them all aboard *Anna*. Hit that place like a whirlwind, totally overwhelm them, steal everything we can, and then run like hell."

"So you're taking the whole piracy thing to heart?" Markus spoke up. "Like in a bad vid?"

She turned and speared him with a serious eye.

"Dude, I'm trying to figure out what kind of pirate hat I need to have made," she replied.

That got a laugh, but it was half-hearted. They knew she was serious.

The locals might later identify the raider as *Anna's Vindication*, but in Siobhan's heart, the vessel was always going to be *Queen Anne's Revenge*. And she was about to introduce them to a bad-ass, lady-pirate named *Blackbeard*.

# THE PROFESSOR (APRIL 17, 402)

Professor Kosnett.

That was how Phil had started thinking of himself. This whole disaster had turned into the sort of extended training exercise that made or broke careers in the Navy. A place where the grading was done on a curve, but so was a fast drive along a cliff edge.

He entered the larger conference room and found himself in what his mind insisted on calling a pirate conclave.

Siobhan and Trinidad, off the prize. Kam and Bok, up from engineering. Heather as the Tactical expert. Evan as the sensors genius.

And Professor Kosnett, attempting to herd goldfish.

Except here, it looked like his job was going to involve pulling on the reins, when a team of semi-wild horses wanted to go like hell. Another job for a command centurion. It was way easier slowing a motivated crew than to kick a lackadaisical one into motion.

Everyone paused as he entered, faces turned expectantly towards him. Silence fell jaggedly.

Phil took the empty seat at the head of the table, feeling

like Zeus overseeing the arguments that would lead to the Trojan War, among the various Olympians. Hopefully, nobody would need to get zapped by a lightning bolt today, because Siobhan Skokomish, with skin almost the color of night, and curly brown hair starting to get long and kinky, had a look in those dark brown eyes that reminded him of nothing so much as Pallas Athena, Goddess of Wisdom and Warfare.

He sat and silently placed both hands palm down on the table top. He hadn't bothered to bring a tablet computer in here. Either one of them would show him something on a local projection, or they could use the big one overhead.

Professor Kosnett was here to grade the first term papers turned in. There were still more papers later, and a final exam ahead, but they had begun.

He decided to throw them a curveball, finding Trinidad Mildon at the far end of the table.

"Is security going to be an issue, with all of your people off-vessel, Centurion?" he asked with a hard glare. Zeus, Lord of All.

Trinidad blinked rapidly. Good.

"If we have a spy or anarchist aboard this vessel, Phil, they've kept a remarkably low-profile to date," Trinidad replied. "I have six because the regulations for a vessel this size indicate six. And we're about to do the thing that is our reason for being here: initiate ground combat with an enemy force. Navin Crncevic's just going to be mad when he hears about it, that we went off and did this without him."

That got a laugh. Navin the Black was notorious for wanting to do more boarding actions. Against pirates or *Fribourg*, it even made a terrible sort of sense. *Buran's Sentient* warships could escape too easily, or blew themselves up rather than being captured. Jessica had done the nigh-impossible by knocking one out long enough to kill the AI and capture the ship intact.

And any *Sentient* warship they ran into out here would eat *CS-405* alive, one bite at a time.

Phil nodded. Just about exactly what he expected, but that just meant that Trinidad was thinking well ahead. All of them were. It was up to the professor to listen and guide. Or Zeus to cast someone down from Mount Olympus.

"Siobhan," he turned next to the head pirate. "Why a mining colony? The gender breakdown is heavily skewed towards strong, able-bodied males, the kind that can cause lots of trouble for raiders."

"And who are almost all generally confined to barracks over at the mine," she replied with a diamond-bright gleam in those dark eyes. "The city itself, according to Kiel's notes, actually leans female, presumably young women looking for a husky, hunky husband grown rich in the mines."

She paused long enough to project the city map onto the tabletop: starport on Phil's port side, mine to starboard.

"I had considered if *405* could get low enough in the atmosphere to take pot-shots at the mine itself with the Type-1's, but the risks are too great," she continued. "And there's not much there to kill, other than dump trucks that look like they weigh almost as much as *Anna*. I propose a strike team of a dozen or so on the ground, with a fast hit and fade, rather than trying to hold the city. Steal a truck or three, load them up with goods, and either drive them right onto *Anna*'s lower deck, or take the time to unload them and maybe go back for more, depending on the locals. We don't know about gendarmes or army forces. Kiel never concerned herself with staging a planetary assault."

"I'll let her know," Phil said dryly, eliciting laughs from the group. "Make sure you update those notes, on the assumption we'll be giving them back the ship later on."

More laughs. At least the group was motivated.

"Should we be close by?" Phil continued. "*405* has the one administrative shuttle, which we could land much closer to a target warehouse, after you have secured the ground defenses. Or were you planning to shift the prize physically into the city?"

That got a blank look from all of them. Followed by furious eyeblinks from Siobhan, and a crocodile grin.

"I keep thinking too small, Phil," she exclaimed. "Thank you. I'm following proper navigational procedures and not racking up parking fines. Yes, we should definitely drop the shuttle closer, probably to this park here."

She pointed at the spot the Professor had already identified, a field that looked like a set of four rugby pitches put together. Phil had no idea what *Buran* did for athletic sports, but they would involve team events, and not individual things, such as track and field. That much he knew about *The Holding*.

"Remember," he said. "Everyone. We are polite to Lan and Kiel, because they are just innocents here. That is a military target, so any resistance it generates is an excuse to blow things up. Keller's mission statement to us is *to materially damage the economy of this sector*. After we stop at the usual orbital truck-stop and steal everything we want, we'll blow it up as well."

"Then, yes," Siobhan said. "I would greatly appreciate it if *405* snuck close during the raid itself, providing us orbital coverage because we'll be blind down there, and an administrative shuttle as a second transport, either for more loot, or in case something goes wrong."

Professor Kosnett nodded. He glanced at Heather, heretofore silent, and got affirmation from her.

It dawned on Phil that he had suddenly become something of a Fleet Centurion by job description, if not rank. He was commanding a squadron now, and not just a single, lightly-armed escort.

He wondered what First Lord Naoumov was going to say, when he next saw her. Petia had once promised him a cruiser command, back before the first war ended and budgets suddenly got tight. All that had been available when it came time was a scout.

And now he might be becoming a pirate warlord.

Phil laughed inside as he listened to the rest of Siobhan's plan.

# HOLDING THE FORT (APRIL 19, 402)

KAM WAS WATCHING over the secondary JumpDrive like a mother hen with a single chick, while wolves howled in the distance. Bok and his teams hadn't even bothered replacing the outer casings since they ended up spending nearly as much time inside, tracing wires that burned out and tuning things, as they did actually flying.

Still, *the little engine that could* had gotten them this far. Creator willing, it would get them the rest of the way, if they could keep it from overheating constantly, and didn't run out of wire when various power surges cooked things.

There was one more jump today, and then hopefully they would have several hours of calm while the raiders did their stuff, down on the planet. And then tomorrow, everything would be holding just fine when they needed to escape.

Yeoman Tuason approached with a tablet in one hand, probably needing her signature on something. By this point, she was considering just making them keep a log of all the times they had to go outside training and regulations in order to fix something or strip something else for parts. The College of Engineers was either going to pin a medal on her chest, or drum her right out of the service, when this was all done.

"Sir?" Galin said as he got close, holding the computer out.

She took it and quick-scanned the request. She stopped and looked up sharply.

"This says you want to take the primary JumpSail controller completely apart, Yeoman," she challenged him.

"Yes, sir," he replied, almost sheepishly.

Tuason was a man of average height, but extremely skinny compared to the rest of the engineers. But he was sharp, or Bok would have never let him stand watches, especially not with the Old Man himself over on Siobhan's prize, getting ready to assault an enemy planet.

"And?" she said.

"So the fire cooked most of the controllers, sir," he began carefully. "Without those, we can't hold a matrix together. But a lot of the hardware itself, the grav-generator and such, might have survived, or at least be in good enough shape that we could fix things. We just gotta get all the way down inside where we can look."

"What's it gain us?" she asked, seeing possibly where he was going. "And why now?"

"The emergency system was never intended to be used for as long as we're going to ride it, sir," Galin replied. "You're just supposed to limp to the nearest system and call for help. Drydock comes, fixes your JumpSail, and all is well. But the grav-generator on the backup is tiny, and overheats pretty easy. If enough pieces of the primary survived, we might be able to use that grav-generator instead, and maybe the cooling system, too. That would get us a longer flight time, and probably better control in JumpSpace itself. Right now, we kinda have to fly straight to a destination, drop out, and then tack into the wind when we go back in. That's why the prize can outrun us everywhere. They don't have cooling and tuning thrown in on top of the jumps."

"And you think this will work?" she pressed.

Galin earned several gold stars for himself when he shrugged, rather than stating a categorical affirmative.

"We aren't using it right now," he offered. "And it's already partway opened up. Had the idea in the shower this morning, when my hot water allotment suddenly ran out 'cause I wasn't paying attention. Asked myself where I could get more heat, and the brain kinda went sideways from there. Would've asked Bok, but he's already busy. Figured I'd ask you. Worst you can say is no."

"Oh, no, Yeoman," she smiled evilly at him. "The worst I can say is *yes*. But this goes on top of your other duties, because I can't spare you from watches, particularly with a team off-boat. Figure out who else you need and let me know when you get the system fully cracked open. Then we'll see if I go to Phil and ask him to let us turn engineering into a rat's nest of cables and hawsers everywhere."

She signed the form and grinned at him. Galin had a look like he was having second thoughts, but if his idea worked, he would get lots of gold stars in the log. Might even decide he wanted to be a Centurion, one of these days. Yeomen like him got to pick if they would become Chiefs or Centurions, if they were good enough.

Galin Tuason probably was, if he wanted to keep showing initiative like this.

Now Kam just had to hold all the moving parts together long enough to get the ship home.

# BLACKBEARD (APRIL 20, 402)

"*Barnaul* Flight Control, this is Commercial Freighter *DYWXK-345029*, *Ukok* Registry, common name *Anna's Vindication*. Requesting a landing window," Siobhan said carefully, hoping her accent wasn't too horrible. *Ukok* was a long ways from here, just barely still in the *Altai* Sector. And the registry number actually matched up with another freighter and a different common name, in Kiel's extensive records of the competition. Markus had done a great job taking apart the transponder and making it programmable.

With any luck, she could fool the locals, at least long enough.

Wasn't like she was planning on coming back to this planet, ever again.

The city below was in late afternoon. Hopefully optimum time to catch somebody tired after a long day, and just wanting to go home and have a beer.

*You just tell us a safe flight corridor, and then we become somebody else's problem, landing either tomorrow morning, or, if we're crazy enough, in the dead of night on a non-automated field.*

Siobhan grinned to herself as she waited. The bridge was tiny, so she generally had the place to herself, like now. Bok and Markus would be aft, watching the engines. Trinidad and his team were waiting in her cabin and the medbay for now.

"*DYWXK-345029*, you are cleared," a tired, bored voice finally replied, about the time she was thinking they had missed the first transmission. Guy was not on the ball. "Pick a spot. As you can see, the field is currently empty. What's your cargo?"

Siobhan hit the transmit button that Lan would have, were he here now, sending an inventory file down that had been accurate, three weeks ago.

"Tuna steaks from *Surgut*," she said. "Plus some minor trade goods of the usual type. Looking to open some new markets here."

"Something other than pasta would be nice, *DYWXK-345029*," he said. "Talk to you tomorrow."

"Acknowledged, Flight Control," she said. "Starting our descent now."

"There are no override controls, *DYWXK-345029*," he hastened to add. "And no lights. If you come down now, you are on your own."

"Piece of cake, Flight Control," she let the words drawl out some. Wasn't every pilot a hotshot wanting to show off, even in an antique like *Anna*?

"Stay put after you land, *DYWXK-345029*," he chided. "The office will be closed until an hour after local dawn. We'll make you fill out all the forms then."

"Acknowledged."

Siobhan nearly giggled, once she cut the line. She pressed the PA instead.

"All hands, this is *Lady Blackbeard*," she called out in a merry voice. "According to the nice man on the ground, they are about to roll up the sidewalks and go home for the night. We'll still hit the control tower first, just to make sure and disable anything that needs it, but there might not be anyone there to say hi. Starting the descent now. Everyone remember to potty before we land. Going to be coming in hot and heavy."

She pressed a button and let the autopilot take over the powered glide she had calculated. Not quite pushing the envelope, because she didn't want to alarm anyone down there, but the fastest path down, to give them the most hours on the ground before the sun came up.

*One crazy pirate babe, coming your way,* Barnaul.

---

THE LANDING FIELD was a perfect square, seven kilometers along the sides, lined up exactly on the longitude and latitude. Plenty of space for megafreighters wanting to haul off ore, since they hadn't built a smelter here to handle industrial loads of things.

Siobhan always wondered why that wasn't the second thing you built, after you dug your first hole in the ground. Of course, if the fools at *Thuringwell* had done the same thing, it wouldn't be a Republic world today. Probably just more efficient to have a huge facility centrally located, most likely in a low planetary orbit somewhere, where the effort to transship ore across deep space wasn't that much more expensive than just hauling the rock up the gravity well for processing in the first place.

Folks here looked too cheap, anyway. Mostly-flat field smushed even more flat by massive ships landing. Not a single light anywhere except for those marking the tower and the gate. No roads at all, which suggested low-flying repulsorlift trucks, once you got it out of the ground and ready for transport. Plus those stupidly-huge dump trucks with ten-meter wheels.

The monstrous sea of tailing piles on the south side of the pit testified to how much raw rock wasn't even worth melting down somewhere. Most systems had some level of asteroid belts, composed of iron and nickel in moon-scale amounts. Doing a pit mine meant that someone had found something rare and valuable, reasonably close to the surface.

After that bastard *Buran* had bombed *St. Legier*, Siobhan was just sorry she didn't have a small nuclear weapon or two to drop in the middle of the mine and render everything five times more expensive to dig out.

But that was an issue to discuss at a later date. Today, she needed to think like a pirate babe.

The bridge was cozy as she dropped the last five thousand meters out of the night sky, swooping in on her target zone from the horizon like an owl spying a mouse in the grass. Trinidad had the other seat for now. She would be joining the raiders and leaving two of Bok's men here to guard the ship shortly.

Tactical Officer meant she was in charge on the ground, in combat. And had programmed an escape flight back to orbit, in case something happened and she didn't make it back.

"All hands, thirty seconds to ground," she said into the PA. "Front bay doors will open as soon as we're sure nobody's shooting at us."

She figured she could get to within a couple hundred meters of the tower and attached office building without causing anyone to wake up. There was a small moon in the sky overhead, just far enough above the horizon right now that they could see by moonlight.

Beside her, Trinidad drew his pistol, checked it one last time, and holstered it again. She figured it was a security blanket kind of thing, since that was the fifth time she had seen him do it since they left orbit.

She glanced over.

"Showtime," he muttered, grinning back at her.

Honestly, it looked like someone else was home, behind those eyes. Hopefully not a berserker. She wanted a quiet night.

Siobhan passed them over the far fence, zipped across the field barely high enough to clear non-existent trees, and slammed the thrusters into reverse. *Anna* dropped on six legs, like the galaxy's biggest scarab, and settled down to feed on the night grass.

"*Barnaul* Flight Control, this is Commercial Freighter *DYWXK-345029*," she called over a low-powered radio. No sense in waking anyone up over at the mine, if she didn't have to. "We've landed."

Nothing.

So far, so good.

Siobhan linked the incoming channel to the PA, so the two men left behind could hear any calls, and then linked her helmet comm to the same channel, so she could pretend to be on the bridge or half-asleep if anybody actually answered.

She rose a beat behind Trinidad and followed him down the steps to the main hallway. Like him, she was wearing a suit of field armor: segmented plates protecting the torso; other bits covering shoulders, arms, hips, and knees; greaves and bracers; boots and gloves. Everything was in marine green, as they liked to call it, including the helmet on her head and the holster for the pulse pistol.

At the bottom of the first steps, Trinidad turned sharply and headed down another flight to the cargo deck, with her fast on his heels.

The team waited there for her to give the command,

lined up in two columns by the big mouth that would open like a ramp. Bok had moved the last few tons of tuna to the aft portion of the bay and dropped a bulkhead wall down to seal that area off. They could still open the aft bay doors from the outside if they needed in, but the tuna would move to *CS-405* soon enough. That kept everything frozen, while most of the front was a staging area for a small planetary invasion.

The kind Keller's squadron was getting to be famous for.

Siobhan counted noses, including Nakisha with the big rifle and Bok with a heavy toolbox on repulsor lifters, so that he could break into anything.

"We are three hundred and twenty meters to the tower," she said as she got in front of the right hand line, next to Trinidad. "Lights are off in the windows. Nobody is answering on the comm. Everyone set?"

Nods and growls answered her. Hungry, angry, and ambitious. The best kind of pirates.

"Opening the doors now," Siobhan said, slapping the big, red lock button with a palm.

It began to beep, and then moved, pivoting away from her and letting the smell of *Barnaul* into the room. Dry. Almost desiccated. Vaguely burnt, but without the warm taste of cinnamon bread underneath it that she always seemed to smell in a desert.

Warm, too. Middle of the night here and still above thirty degrees. She could only imagine what it would be like closer to the equator or in the middle of the day. Place felt kinda nasty, which might be why there were so few colonists here.

Maybe you had to be desperate to take a job like this.

The ramp grounded with a ping. Trinidad was already moving, so Siobhan went off two steps behind him. No way in hell she was going to run across this field, but she figured she could maybe jog with the marines. They trained for this sort of thing constantly.

Siobhan just did her kilometers on the treadmill and the elliptical.

Like all strange planets, the night sky was a confusing puzzle. None of the patterns she was used to, and far enough across the galaxy that none of the stars she knew were probably even visible from here.

The city in the distance was lit, however poorly. Frontier town feel, if you could call it that. Lights on a few of the buildings towards the center. More sparse, the farther you got away. At least there were no farm houses out this way.

And the ground was level enough that she wasn't the first person to face-plant, tripping over something. Max got that honor. At least he hadn't broken anything, when they got him upright.

Finally, they struggled over to the building. Well, she struggled. It wasn't fair that Bok wasn't even breathing heavy, let alone the six marines.

"We figure the door's got an alarm?" Trinidad asked, pointing at the front.

"If there is one, that's where I'd put it," Bok answered. "Probably better to take out a window and go through that way."

"I agree," Siobhan said. "Smash a window."

Bok pulled a telescoping prybar from his toolkit, snapped it fully open, and stepped close to the big window that let office workers watch the sunrise.

"Always wanted to do this," he said, swinging with both hands.

The material was some sort of safety glass. Silicon based, but covered over with a polymer layer of some sort. It fractured into pieces no bigger than her fingernail, but only a tiny number of those fell into the room.

"Oh? That's how it's going to be?" he growled.

Siobhan chuckled as he shifted his stance. Nothing like an engineer thwarted when he wanted to break something.

This blow was flat, aimed at a corner of the now-broken glass, just above the frame. There was a LOT of torque involved, especially as strong as Bok was. And as angry.

This shot took out most of the glass from the bottom half. A reverse blow finished it off.

One of the marines, Siobhan thought it was Gerry, but she couldn't tell with the helmets and armor, squatted down outside the window, presenting a knee and holding out a hand.

She watched the other five marines use the knee as a step, and the hand up as a brace, and each hopped into the dark room beyond, flashlights on helmets lighting things up as they moved, guns tracking like bloodhounds.

"Sir?" the marine called to her next, so Siobhan went in.

She didn't bother drawing a gun. If the five in front of her couldn't handle whatever came up, there was little she could do to help.

Instead, she pointed to an interior door, currently closed. It looked like a utility closet. Felt like one, in any case.

Bok was beside her now, watching the marines clear the building professionally in two pairs.

"What's in there, you suppose?" Siobhan pointed.

"One way to find out," Bok smiled.

Siobhan fell in with Bok and his two engineers. He walked right up to the door and tried to turn the lock, but it didn't move.

"Worth a try," he said, with a laugh.

One of the engineers rapped loudly on the hinges, visible on this side of the door.

"Yup," Bok agreed. "Pop 'em and let's see what we've got."

Siobhan could tell that she'd spent too much time in space, around powered hatches and airlocks. She watched in confusion that turned to awe as the man pulled out a simple screwdriver, drove it into the bottom of the hinge, and popped a pin out the top with his fist. He did the same with the other one, and Bok just pulled the door out of the frame by the handle.

"Ah," the Boatswain laughed, looking in. "That's what we're looking for."

Siobhan lined her helmet light up with the small closet. Sure enough, an electrical panel filled one section of the wall.

"Security team," she said over the local radio. "We've found the breakers for the building. Stand by while we shut everything off. Emergency lights may come on in your area."

Bok stepped up and ran one big mitt down the line of breakers, snapping them off with cracks like lightning. Around her, Siobhan watched terminals and comm gear go dark.

"Top, found a motor pool," a female voice said over the comm. Nakisha, probably.

"Where?" Siobhan answered.

"North east corner, ground floor," came the answer.

Siobhan managed to be a step faster than Bok and his men this time.

"Tower level secured," came another man's voice. Vladimir, she thought. "Building uninhabited. All automated systems appear to be shut down."

"Join us at the motor pool," Trinidad's voice came on the line. "All hands."

It wasn't much, when she got there. One smaller sedan, a four-seater that looked like the sort of thing visiting inspectors got hauled around in. The other vehicle was more to her liking.

It was a big, battered flatbed, riding on two, massive

banks of repulsors, with a small cab for two people, and a space six meters wide and nearly twenty long in back. Looked like a gray dragon crossed with a barroom brawler. A long, blue tarp was folded up on the bed and tied down, like an opera cape.

"Markus, you drive," Bok called as they got close.

"I'm rated on equipment this size," Nakisha shot back across the radio.

"You'll be in back if you need to shoot at people," Siobhan overrode the woman's complaint. "I'm in the cab with Markus, everyone else under the tarp and tie it down loosely enough that you're covered, but can still shoot if you have to. Nobody fires until Trinidad or I give the order."

This whole adventure was starting to feel like driving a ground vehicle up an icy hill. Once you got going, it was necessary to maintain your momentum, or you might slide back. *CS-405* was in orbit, watching, so nobody could sneak up on them that way, but there was a whole planet of potential trouble down here.

Now, she just had to break into that warehouse without attracting attention.

# BURGLARS (APRIL 20, 402)

TRINIDAD SUPPOSED the city was also called *Barnaul*, at least until the population got big enough to have two towns. Maybe they just called it *The Town*.

He didn't feel like stopping a random pedestrian to ask. People might get the wrong idea, considering his armor. Instead, he kept low, riding under the big blanket like a warm, happy piglet. One with a gun in hand. Nakisha was watching the other side. Their feet were just touching under the blanket so a silent kick could get his attention if trouble broke out.

Trinidad kept his opinions to himself about how much better a driver Markus was over Nakisha. Engineers tended to be careful when moving heavy equipment. Most of the time, Nakisha drove like Death was on her heels and gaining ground.

*Barnaul* was a dreary place. Or whatever the city they were driving through was called. At least this part of it, anyway. Trinidad could see an area more lit-up, about a kilometer over from the side street/alley where they suddenly halted and grounded the big truck. From the map in his head, that was the main square for town, bounded by the government building, mine offices, and a big department store that served most of the town's needs.

Right now, Trinidad figured they were in the industrial quarter. Concrete slab walls in all directions, with a marked lack of graffiti, told him he wasn't home in *Aquitaine*. He couldn't imagine this much canvas not attracting some budding talent. Or a busybody government turning it all into murals celebrating whatever they valued.

*Buran* was too efficiency-minded to waste money on making things pretty. At least this far out on some forgotten frontier, away from the more civilized places, where Scholars might take a different view.

A door opened. A second. Siobhan appeared in his line of sight. She paused to look both directions, and up.

"All clear," she said quietly.

Meercats boiled out of their den at the words, bodies flowing down the sides of the flatbed, guns pointed all directions.

He had good people.

Trinidad looked quickly around and figured the Director of Photography would probably put his cameras *there*. Out of the way and with good exposure to all the action. Bad guys would probably come from *that direction*. Accidental bystander would probably appear around *that other corner*.

Quickly, Trinidad laid out coverage zones for his people, taking advantage of the script in his head and hoping this turned into a caper instead of a car chase.

Behind him, Siobhan and Bok conferred in quiet tones, safely inside the cocoon of armed men and women with lots of guns. Trinidad tapped Nakisha to join them inside. She was only a First-Rate-Spacer, but that was just time-in-grade. He could see her as a Yeoman in another year, and maybe a Centurion like him, a few after that.

A thought pulled Trinidad into the conversation the inside team was having.

"We're supposed to do maximum damage to the enemy, right?" he asked quietly.

"That's right," Siobhan answered. "Just about to ask Bok for something to set a fire, once we get everyone out we want."

"Nakisha," Trinidad said louder, getting her attention. "You've got a thermal, right?"

"Yes, sir," she barked quietly, grinning ear to ear. "Two."

"There you go," Trinidad said. "Not enough to burn concrete walls, but more than enough to go all pyromaniac, whenever you want."

"Perfect," Siobhan exclaimed. "Bok, get your boys to work opening that door."

"On it," the Boatswain said, dragging Markus along.

Trinidad went back to the side of the truck, thought about it for a moment, and climbed up onto the flatbed. He judged heights and distances.

Yeah, that will work.

Markus had parked close to a warehouse wall, just past the spot where they could roll the garage door up and load the bed easily.

"Gerry, up and give me a hand," Trinidad called, climbing up onto the roof of the cab next.

Gerry was there a moment later.

"What've you got, boss?" he asked.

"You brace feet here and hands on the side of the building," Trinidad said. "I'll climb your back, and that gets me to the roof to provide enfilading fire if we need it."

Gerry nodded and leaned against the concrete wall like this was a detective show and he had just gotten busted by the good guys. Trinidad hid his chuckle, holstered his pistol, and went up the man's back like a boy squirrel chasing a girl in the spring.

From Gerry's shoulders, he could just reach the top, but not get leverage higher.

"Gerry, I need a hand up," he said quietly.

Gerry shifted all his weight to the left side and pulled his right hand back. Trinidad felt the palm go under his boot and grip hard.

"Ready?" Gerry called with a grunt.

"Go."

Gerry's arm straightened out and nearly shotputted Trinidad onto the roof. The marine wasn't all that bright, but he could probably take even someone as strong as Bok, seven falls in ten in Greco-Roman wrestling.

"Good," Trinidad said. "I've got the roof. Shift yourselves around some to cover without me down there."

Trinidad watched for a moment to make sure they had it under control, and then moved to a different side.

The roof up here was slanted maybe five degrees from a center beam. Just enough to cause rain to run off instead of pooling. Probably to keep the dust and sand from accumulating, considering how hot it must get around here. Didn't look like it ever rained. A meter-tall wall ran around the outside like a balcony railing, providing him a solid barrier in case somebody opened fire. Or a balustrade to land on, in the middle of a good hand-to-hand fight sequence.

Except he'd need a camera up in the air to catch the view just right. Maybe next time.

Hell, if this was going to be an ongoing thing, maybe they needed exactly that, a camera drone, low-profile, that someone could fly around and see beyond corners.

Trinidad made a note to ask Bok to build him something. Or Markus. The crazy redneck would probably see that as a challenge, working with so few correct parts and needing to improvise.

Trinidad took up an overwatch spot with a good view of the approaching main street and watched. The truck was in a side lot, out of sight. Hopefully, out of mind.

# FELONY BREAKING AND ENTERING
## (APRIL 20, 402)

SIOBHAN FINALLY UNDERSTOOD Trinidad's nervous twitch, drawing his weapon and checking the charge every few minutes. It gave him something to do while he waited on other people doing things.

She caught herself rocking back and forth while Markus and Bok worked. The faceplate was off the panel beside the door, exposing part of a circuit board and wires, with low voices and a few gestures with tools.

There was nothing for her to do. She almost drew her own pistol to check it, but stopped herself in time. That was Trinidad's thing. She would just have to come up with her own nervous habit. Flexing every finger in sequence, outer to inner, seemed to soothe her nerves.

Bok grunted a rude profanity. Markus sliced a wire, and the door suddenly retracted into the wall like a starship hatch.

"We're in," Markus said over his shoulder.

Nakisha materialized from nowhere, before Siobhan could take even a step, a green and black ghost with a rifle pointed at the floor.

"Me, first," she insisted.

Siobhan nodded and squeezed a quick fist. Now would finally be the time to draw the pistol.

She left the safety on anyway.

Inside, the ceiling vaulted to something like seven meters. High enough for a second story, but none had been added. Instead, rack shelving dominated the space, full of metal shipping crates that seemed to come in three distinct sizes, the biggest of which looked to be a matched fit for the bed of the truck out front.

Probably a *Buran* standard she would need to master at some point. She could see stealing the truck by just driving it and a cargo right up the ramp of *Anna* and flying away. Future raids would be a lot easier if the team came with their own transport.

The blast of cold air in her face was a shock, after the night's heat. Solid, concrete walls insulated pretty well, especially with cladding on the inside. The air temperature here seemed to be about eight degrees above zero. In her ear, her armor's system clicked loudly and beeped, letting her know that the cooling system had just changed its mind and cranked the heat up instead.

Proofed against weather, Siobhan followed Nakisha inside.

The warehouse went on forever. Siobhan hadn't taken long blocks into account when mapping this place, realizing intellectually now that this was two, square, long blocks under a single roof. And this was the smaller warehouse, mostly dedicated to refrigerated and frozen goods, which meant foodstuffs for the most part, plus liquefied gases. She had a note to herself to grab a few bottles of compressed oxygen for welding and such, if they came across them. Also useful to supplement the life support system.

None of the crates were painted with contents on the outside, just bar codes. But she had been prepared for that.

"Find me the shipping office," she said out loud.

Nakisha moved deeper into the vast space, Siobhan in her wake.

There seemed to be something over there, about midway down this last aisle. At least the shelving ended in a wall of some sort. A walk would be nice, given how her breath fogged in here, but Siobhan wasn't sure about the dry, metallic taste to the air.

The world's biggest walk-in refrigerator, although it paled next to the one back on *Anameleck Prime* where the Navy staged things for Home Fleet. She'd served a quick stint there while originally waiting for the orders that got her to First Expeditionary Fleet.

Behind her, Siobhan could hear Bok and Markus at work on the controls for the garage door. It rolled up suddenly. A few moments later, the flatbed backed in through the door in a welter of roars and beeps, but they were muted at this distance.

Siobhan glanced back as she joined Nakisha at what looked like an interior office block, probably insulated and heated for workers to be in short sleeves. Most of the group was outside or by the door, leaving only Nakisha with her, and Dedra Janowski.

"Door's unlocked," Nakisha said. "Ready?"

Siobhan pointed her gun in the right direction and nodded.

The marine pulled it open suddenly on silent hinges.

Warm air bled out.

Yup. Office.

They were through and closed the door quickly. Siobhan's suit chirped again and went neutral with the HVAC controls. At least until she started moving again and got overheated.

Unlike the *Fribourg Empire*'s fetish for paper records, *Buran* was all electronic. The room had no filing cabinets at all, just a series of workstations, plus a long, chest-high counter, presumably where folks came in when they wanted to pick up goods in storage, or drop them off.

Siobhan crossed to one of the workstations and pressed a button on the keyboard. The screen lit up for a username and password.

*Crap. Like I'm going to know that?*

So much for only stealing good stuff.

Siobhan huffed and was just about to go have Bok start cracking cases when Dedra stopped her.

"What are you doing?" Siobhan asked as the second woman opened the top drawer, rifled around some, and pulled out a small notepad.

Nakisha Onks was covering the front door, out onto the street, with a mean-looking rifle.

"Here," Dedra said, holding the pad up. "Try this."

The pad had random characters scrawled on several lines, all but the last one crossed out.

"Seriously?" Siobhan asked. "Who does that?"

"Someone who hates facing a ninety-day password cycle," Dedra grinned. "Got a few of them back on the ship. When I'm feeling mean, I cross out a line and add a new one without saying anything. Then they put the wrong one in three times and lock themselves out."

"You're evil," Siobhan noted.

"Guilty as charged."

But that turned out to be the password for the last person to log in here. The screen lit up.

"What in all hells is that?" Dedra asked, peeking over Siobhan's shoulder as Siobhan sat and typed.

"Mongolian," Siobhan said. "*Anna*'s all Mongolian, these days, so we have to read it as well as speak it."

She quickly toggled through a few menu items.

"Here we go," she muttered out loud. "Chickens, cleaned and frozen. One for every pot."

She selected the icon and watched the screen flip happily to an internal map of the facility.

"Need me?" Dedra asked.

"Nope," Siobhan replied. "Bok will, shortly."

The woman nodded and trotted out the front door.

"Bok," Siobhan called on the radio. "Aisle Four. Section seven. Big container."

She read the shipping number, waited for his acknowledgement, and went digging for the next container. The chicken was in one of the big boxes, so it would fill the truck, but *Anna* had an overhead crane that could unload it.

She considered the timing, but things were looking good. She would send half the team back to *Anna* to quickly unload the cargo, and then find something else to steal here.

There was a whole warehouse of goodies awaiting her.

―――――

By the time Markus got back with the empty truck, Siobhan had already found the next candidate for grand theft. Another big crate, this time filled with frozen milk solids. Siobhan didn't cook, but Nakisha had assured her that it was the basis of something called a mother sauce, and that Jules would kiss them all for bringing it back. Especially with lots of chickens that he could use to make stock.

*You made chicken stock from used bones?*

It had been just over an hour since they first cracked the outer door. Siobhan wanted to get greedy, but there were limits to how much space *Anna* had right now, and the one admin shuttle coming down from orbit didn't have a crane, so they would have to steal a couple of powered sleds here, and then hand-load the truck with small boxes.

She settled for several meter-sized cubes of juice concentrate, more meat, and whatever small boxes Bok thought they could cram onto the big truck and still have space for the crew to ride. The end of Aisle Three, closest to the garage door, looked like angry beavers had gnawed at it, holes showing up everywhere in the previously-organized shelves, with boxes like wood scraps on the concrete floor.

The boxes were all insulated, and the design was plugged into the shelf to power onboard systems that kept the contents at a precise temperature. Siobhan figured more rednecking, when they got back, to run two big power cables to the big boxes she was keeping for now.

Kam would have to break out every extension cable she could find, or just empty the boxes into the fridge up on the ship and break the boxes down. Bunch of good control systems suddenly available for repurposing.

Out of space to store her stolen goods, Siobhan had closed down the workstation and left the office area, but not before adding a new row to someone's password list and crossing out the real one. Dedra was evil, but a little juvenile delinquency really made Siobhan laugh, on top of *Felony Breaking and Entering*, plus *Burglary* and *Grand Theft*.

Just as she and Nakisha exited the office, Trinidad's voice came over the radio.

"Possible trouble incoming," he said quietly. "All hands stand by for gendarmes."

Come to think of it, she hadn't seen him since they arrived. Must have stayed outside the whole time, supervising his fire teams.

She was just glad he was on the ball.

"How many?" Siobhan asked, starting to jog.

Nakisha went by her at a dead run, but the marine chick was like that. All of them were.

"One land vehicle," Trinidad replied. "Basic patrol car, but on wheels instead of repulsors. I can see one deputy driving."

"Everyone hold fire until my order," Siobhan called, upping her speed. "Trinidad, try to take him prisoner quietly. Everyone hide where you are. Make him come inside the building where we can ambush him."

"Like a bad horror movie, boss," Trinidad said earnestly.

Seriously, that boy was strange. Must be not coming up from the ranks, or going to the Academy. The things he said.

Still, the man went beyond competent. And had a whole team of crazy marines with him, plus Old Man Bok and a couple of his folks.

Siobhan decided to listen to her own orders. She faded into one of the gaps in Aisle Three, tucked back out of immediate sight, but with a good view through the shelves to the garage door.

As she watched, Markus piled out of the cab and scampered for cover on Aisle Two.

The place was suddenly deserted. Kinda even felt like a bad vid, right after the monster had snuck into a warehouse like this and was lying in wait for the gendarme with the flashlight.

Siobhan found herself peeking backwards, into the darker areas of the silent and eerie warehouse, just to make sure nothing was sneaking up on her right now.

*Damn you, Trinidad. I did not need that in my head right now.*

She took a deep breath and concentrated on stretching her fingers, one after the other. Now was not the time to draw the pistol and be fiddling with it. Probably drop it on the concrete. Or fire a shot into the ceiling accidentally.

"Okay, he's parked the vehicle at the intersection," Trinidad said. "Turning on the spotlight now."

Sure enough, Siobhan saw lights paint the open garage door, winking off the front of the truck, currently loaded with the big crate of milk solids, plus half a dozen smaller crates piled precariously atop that. Markus would need to exit the garage doors carefully to keep from scraping everything off the top.

Siobhan made a note not to have anyone up there until the thing was outside.

"He's on the radio now," Trinidad's commentary continued. "We may be blown, if he's calling for reinforcements. Stand by."

Another comm circuit chimed suddenly.

"*Team Anna*, this is Heather Lau aboard *405*," the woman suddenly said. "Evan is reading local communications with our sensors. Stand by for his relay."

Seriously, *405* could listen in on a low-powered police radio from orbit?

Siobhan had always concentrated on flying. But they were a scout, with two monstrously-huge sensor arrays at the ends of the ship, where other corvettes had their Type-3-Tuned beams. Maybe there was something to all the sneakiness a scout could be.

"Beel, looks like someone broke into the warehouse," a man's voice said in a weary tone. "Probably another bored drunk on a dare."

"Understood, Mohr," another local replied, choppy with signal attenuation. "Check it out, but be careful, especially if they're drunk. If I don't hear back in five minutes, I'll send the cavalry."

"Thank you, Beel."

"All hands," Trinidad took up the narrative. "Vehicle in

motion. Now he's parking in the lot out front. Anybody up in the office?"

"Negative, Trinidad," Siobhan answered. "We've cleared out and are in the main facility."

"Roger that," he whispered over the line. "Deputy is out of the vehicle, parked right up at the corner. Seen enough bad movies in his time, too. One hand on an undrawn sidearm, other hand holding a billy club with a flashlight at the end. Checking the office. Taking his time. Now he's walking down to the corner. Everybody duck now."

Siobhan felt herself do the same, and cursed. That boy had a great radio voice. Compelling.

"Okay, he seems satisfied," the whispers continued. "Sneaking down the side of the building with the light off and the gun drawn. Wants to make an entrance. Everyone inside now."

This was where being in command was nice. Siobhan just had to stay here and let folks like Nakisha, Trinidad, and Bok handle things. Poor cop was outnumbered eight to one right now, if they moved quickly on him.

Siobhan saw the officer slip around the corner of the door, pistol pointed at the cab of the truck, probably expecting to find a laughing drunk trying to make off with something. So far, the man was acting utterly professional. He walked to the side of the truck, climbed up on the running boards, and looked inside.

There was nobody home.

Smart guy, he holstered the pistol before he jumped back down, landing rather like a cat.

"Now would be a very good time to surrender, Officer," Nakisha's calm voice floated across the darkness. "Otherwise, we will shoot you."

Slight emphasis on the *we*. Let him know there are odds, and those are bad.

The man froze.

A flashlight on the front rails of a heavy rifle speared the man in its cone. Then a second. And a third.

Hands went very slowly, very deliberately into the air. The universal symbol that transcended languages.

Bok suddenly climbed out from under the truck and took the pistol and flashlight away from the cop. *Under the truck? Where? Okay, whatever.*

Handcuffs were located and utilized. He got set down on a handy crate. The radio got absconded. Siobhan decided to join the group.

"What is all this?" the officer demanded. "Thieves?"

"Pirates," Siobhan corrected him with a hard smile. "The *Imperial Fribourg Fleet* has finally made it as far as *Barnaul.*"

That got through to the man. His golden skin paled considerably.

"This is merely a raid," she continued. "We're not here to drop orbital bombs on your city, like *The Eldest* did to our worlds."

*Not ours, but we're pretending to wear the flag. And buddy, there are a lot of angry people out there. Grand Admiral Wachturm probably would have asked us to burn the city to the ground if he were here.*

But this guy was just a cop, doing his job on a border world filled with miners.

The radio beeped.

"Mohr, how's it looking?" the man apparently known as Beel asked.

Siobhan looked at the truck, already loaded, and did the math.

"Clock's ticking people," she said. "Cut and run time."

Nakisha surprised the hell out of Siobhan by leaning in close and shooting the prisoner in the center of the chest, with his own pistol.

"Damn it, sailor," she snarled angrily. "Did I order that?"

"Stun pistol, Commander?" Nakisha admitted sheepishly, holding it out sideways.

Mohr had slumped over and fallen off the box, but his chest was not currently smoldering.

Siobhan took a deep breath and swallowed the sudden rage. That really was a stun pistol, and it had been a good idea.

Nakisha was using marine-thinking to solve the problem. They did that.

Siobhan had to think bigger.

"Load everything we can, right now," she ordered loudly. "If he's got a stunner, the next folks won't, and we do not need to be trapped here. Markus, get the truck outside now, so we can load things and not worry about clearance. Trinidad, let me know when the next set of lights come. They won't be on this channel, since they'll be assuming we're doing exactly what we are."

"Affirmative, *Team Anna*," Heather's *Goddess-From-The-Skies* broadcast came through. "Evan reports significant radio traffic on a different frequency. Currently, all scrambled and he doesn't think he'll be able to crack it fast enough."

"You heard the woman," Siobhan yelled. "Pack and run."

An ant nest exploded around her, bodies headed every direction.

"Bok," she called. "Anything in here burn?"

He wasn't in sight, but that didn't matter.

"Doubt it," the Boatswain replied over the radio. "Concrete and steel."

"What about the office?" Nakisha Onks came on the line.

"Burn it," Siobhan ordered. "But not until we're ready to leave."

"*Team Anna*, this is Yeoman Yamaguchi, aboard shuttle

*Cherokee*," another voice came in. "I'm close to landing. Should I abort?"

Siobhan had forgotten about him, and the plan to drop in a park nearby. Too many moving parts right now. She would need to do better, if she really wanted to become a pirate.

"Negative on abort, *Cherokee*," she answered. "But shift to secondary zone now and land close to *Anna*. We'll be coming hot with materials to load aboard you, but I'm not sure how quickly the authorities will be onto us. Might be a running chase to the port, so prepare to scramble empty on my order."

"Roger that, *Anna*. Aborting primary now. See you at secondary."

Siobhan took a breath and tried to place all the game pieces in her head. Phil was way better at this, but that was why he was a Command Centurion, and she was just a pilot.

For now.

Markus had the truck in motion, humming politely as it waddled carefully out the garage door, like a pregnant woman.

Load and run, just like that. Nothing Siobhan had seen suggested orbital defenses of any kind.

She jogged towards the door, stepping over Officer Mohr's legs as Dedra dragged him off to safety.

They just had to get away.

# SHOWTIME (APRIL 20, 402)

"Markus, go ahead and park it right there," Trinidad called over the radio, judging the truck's roof and his own athletic abilities. "Just don't leave without me."

"Understood," the engineer replied, setting the big beast down on landing skids with the faintest squeak.

Trinidad found it amusing that most of the conversations on the ground had been in Mongolian, except when they needed to talk to one of the newcomers for whom Mandarin might be a stretch. Then it was English or Bulgarian.

But the crew of *Anna's Vindication* thought and spoke in Mongolian these days.

Awesome, but they might need to add subtitles to the gig at a later date.

Trinidad shifted back around to the corner of the building overlooking the main street out front, the side where they were, and the police car below him.

Thoughts of juvenile delinquency reared their ugly heads as he considered the virgin, concrete walls around here.

"Gerry, this is Trinidad," he said. "Grab a thermal grenade from Nakisha if you don't have one and place it underneath the police cruiser, but don't arm it. Just right under the front bumper like an apple."

"Coming up," Gerry replied, jogging into view like a giant sloth lumbering after the fox in Trinidad's favorite cartoons.

"Nakisha," Trinidad continued. "Your job will be to take the shot at that grenade, after you set the office on fire."

"Going for high score here, boss?" she snarked back at him.

"Chase sequence montage," he answered. "You always need pyrotechnical effects for the bad guys to drive through as they start the chase. Far be it for me to deny them an entrance. Just need some theme music now."

"Asked Heather?" Nakisha laughed.

"No," he said. "Doubt they'd get the joke."

Lights up the road caught his eye suddenly. Vehicles, coming closer at high speed, but silent. Probably thought they were sneaking up on him, or something. He counted noses quickly.

"All hands, we have three vehicles incoming," Trinidad said over the comm. "Marines move to the front corner of the building to lay down suppressing fire. Nakisha, prepare to start your fire inside and then join us here. Gerry, stay with the truck and cover the rear flank."

Gerry was big. And strong. But his forte was close combat. Blades and fists, not rifles. Him covering the rear let him be useful and free up one of the better shots.

Assents over the radio. Trinidad glanced back and watched Siobhan climb up into the cab. Good. Bok and his team didn't need her in the way while loading, and there wasn't much she could do to help at this point. Better to have her thinking, rather than manual labor.

That's what the rest of them were for.

Trinidad found cover behind a vertical pillar about a

quarter of the way along the front wall and became still as the lights approached. The vehicles pulled into the lot near the front door and parked, not quite below him, but not that far off. Half a dozen men and women piled out of the vehicles, some of them pulling on jackets. Two of them were still in civilian gear, probably woken up in the dead of night for a riot.

*Oh, you got no idea, pal.*

Nakisha worked explosives like she drove, right out at the edge of crazy.

The front of the building erupted outwards like the best video games or bank-heist movies, showering the parking lot with broken safety glass and metal bits, in a flash of heat and light, followed by a dull roar.

That crazy marine must have rolled it right up against the front door to get that effect. Trinidad liked it. Made a note to add it to the repertoire, next movie he made with this crew.

The cops on this side of the cars had all been knocked on their asses, but that was mostly surprise and shock, rather than concussion. Thermal grenades didn't throw much shrapnel, and the glass door was going to be tempered and coated, like the control tower had been.

Scary, but not lethal, more like being pelted with hail than bullets.

Trinidad felt like he was in one of those kids cartoons, where good guys and bad guys shoot at each other constantly with pulse weapons and nobody ever got hurt. Just vehicles hit, everyone bails out, and then it crashes in a pretty fireball.

He could work with that sort of a ratings system here.

"All hands, destroy the vehicles," Trinidad ordered, standing up just enough to get a hand and pistol over the parapet. "Keep them pinned, but don't kill anyone. Whoever has the stun pistol, feel free to test the range on it. I want some impressive special effects here."

Laughter on the radio greeted him.

His team knew he was weird. Reveled in it, from what he could tell. Commanders like Navin the Black or Vo Arlo were all spit-polish and angry, most of the time. His people loved starring in adventure vids.

Pulse rifles at this distance were also a lot of fun, when you cranked the charge up for damage, instead of range. Holes started appearing in the sides of the cars accompanied by loud bangs.

The tires were apparently solid rubber, because somebody managed to put three, rapid shots into one and set it on fire, acrid smoke suddenly adding that element of atmosphere that had been missing.

Trinidad realized that this kind of night scene was almost always shot with rain drizzling in the background. He had forgotten.

Need to raid a wetter planet next time.

Or figure out how to generate a sandstorm. The possibilities were both silly, and endless.

The cops were madly scrambling for cover now. They had the trunks of their vehicles open and were pulling out longer firearms to try to engage, suddenly in way over their heads with the situation. Trinidad held his fire and watched. If they didn't know he was here, he could be that drone in the sky filming the fight scene.

Sure enough, one of the women gestured and two of the cops took off at a mad dash for the other end of the building.

"All hands, they have split up to attempt a flank," he said. "Gerry, two coming your way, but they'll be a while circling the whole building. Siobhan, that's probably our cue to call it a night."

"Acknowledged, Trinidad," the commander said. "Make sure the vehicles are too damaged to follow, and then withdraw."

"Everybody concentrate fire on the farthest car," Trinidad said amidst the snaps and pops of fire going both ways. "Put it out of commission now."

"*Anna Team*, this is Heather," the Sky Goddess was back. "Evan reports that the cops on scene have panicked and called for any reinforcements on an open channel. Mine security has responded. Expect more help soon."

Just for verisimilitude, Trinidad opened fire on a cactus ten meters in front of the two cops racing for the flank. Pulse pistol really couldn't set fire to a healthy tree, but the cactus exploded, throwing green, squishy guts everywhere. The two cops threw themselves on the ground with bawls of surprise.

And maybe a few needles stuck in sensitive bits.

Trinidad ducked as the other cops spotted him and opened fire on the building.

For fun, he took one of his normal assault grenades and threw it as hard as he could out into the street well beyond the officers, where it wouldn't hurt anyone.

Assault grenades had no shrapnel at all, designed for clearing the hallway just outside a hostile airlock, but they were loud. And flashy.

The cops panicked some more, probably afraid they had just walked into a planetary invasion and were trapped in the crossfire. One of them apparently opened fire on a hardware store down the block. Trinidad watched the glass façade melt into a river of pieces.

"Boss, we could probably take them," Nakisha called. "They're pinned and pissing their pants over there."

"Negative," he ordered. "We've done all we need to, and they've got help coming. Somebody put an assault grenade right under the nearest car. Everybody else mount up. Nakisha, prepare to kill the first car you're using for cover."

Assents. Bok told his people to forget the rest of the boxes and board.

Trinidad watched Nakisha's little junko bird fly true across the open space, roll to a halt just under the driver's door, and go bang, tossing the car in the air and nearly flipping it over.

That was his cue, as the cops all started to run for better cover. He ran to the corner at a hard jog, holstering his pistol and making sure everyone below was in motion.

"Fire in the hole," Nakisha called as she started to run for the truck.

Markus had the beast up on the repulsors now. Nakisha was running headlong, and got to the back bumper before Trinidad did, but that was okay. She needed to be farther away from the explosion when it went boom.

"Markus, start moving," Trinidad ordered.

"You aboard?" Siobhan called nervously. "I don't see you."

She was checklisting noses out the back window, but she was looking down, not up.

In his head, Trinidad was counting.

The truck rose and started to drift forward, the repulsors fighting the overload Bok had put on the flatbed.

Trinidad bounced up in the air, put his foot down on the concrete balustrade, and leapt into space.

Behind him, the shot would have won the Director of Photography an award, as the thermal grenade went off. Unlike the assault grenade, thermals were all about damage.

The car flipped backwards on its long axis in a tremendous fireball recorded on Gerry's camera, standing perfectly still to capture it. He was good about that.

In the foreground, Trinidad flying across open space, backlit and silhouetted by the flames, as he came down on the cab of the truck.

He had been expecting Markus to be moving faster by now, but hadn't taken mass into account. Instead of spiking the landing, he was about to pitch face first over the front of the vehicle and get run over, when Vlad lashed out like a snake and grabbed his ankle.

For a moment, there was nothing below him but pavement and broken bones. Then that human anchor turned him into a figurehead, breasting the open skies of *Barnaul* and scaring away the bad sea spirits.

"Cut," Nakisha yelled with a laugh. "Print."

Just because he was a marine didn't mean he had ever stopped being an actor.

Besides, they still had to get off this planet.

# RECEDING TIDE (APRIL 21, 402)

Markus had apparently left the front gate to the starport field open on his last run to town. Siobhan could see it propped open now as the truck hurtled at high speed down the rough roadway, an overloaded tortoise with its ass on fire.

*Anna* was dark and invisible from here, as she should be, but *Cherokee* was lit up like a Midwinter tree.

"Yamaguchi," she ordered over the line as they entered the reservation. "Kill all external lights, right now. We know where you are. The bad guys don't need to."

Long pause, and then that lit corner of the field went dark.

Hopefully, whoever was chasing them hadn't put two and two together. The field was completely flat and bare, but in the darkness, both ships were just suggestions rather than neon enticements to come over and party.

If they could gain a few extra minutes to load, there would be that much more stuff to get everyone to the next waypoint. Probably not enough to get them home, but every day got them farther away from bad guys.

One advantage of a repulsor truck was that the pits in the

road got smoothed out. She could only imagine how rough this ride would be with the sorts of solid tires those cops had been using, back when their vehicles worked.

Still, everyone had gotten away unhurt, and they had a head start on Johnny Law catching up. Time to put it to use.

"*405*, this is Siobhan," she tried to sound calm, "What's our company look like?"

"You have two vehicles headed in your direction, *Team Anna*," Heather replied a beat later. "By scale, the front one looks like a riot control van. Think your chassis, with an armored box on it and a turret weapon up top. Can't tell how big the gun is, but they're chasing you."

"What's the second one?" Siobhan asked when she realized Heather had stopped talking suddenly.

"Uhm, that thing's a dump truck, right, Evan?" Heather said, apparently forgetting the line was voice-activated. "Really? Crap."

Now Siobhan was beginning to get nervous.

"*Team Anna*, be advised," Heather continued in a sharp, professional voice. "Second vehicle is a dump truck from the mine. For scale, the tires are ten meters in diameter, and the truck you are currently driving would fit sideways in the bed. Scan suggests that it might outweigh *Anna's Vindication* on pure, empty mass."

Yup. Crap.

"Understood, *405*," Siobhan said. "Anything you can do to slow it down?"

"Negative, Siobhan," Phil's firm voice suddenly came on the line. "We would need a Type-3 tuned just right, to even penetrate that depth of atmosphere. Judge your situation accordingly. You are on your own."

"Can you tell that Bedrov fellow it would be nice to add a single-shot Primary on the nose of the ship?" Siobhan asked. "Turn us into a unicorn or something, even for just one blast."

"Not the worst idea I've heard today, Siobhan," Phil said. "What's your status?"

"Sixty seconds to *Cherokee*," she answered. "Then unloading. We'll just drive the truck onto *Anna* and run, after that."

"Don't stay too long," he chided her. "We don't know if that turret can kill either of you, if he gets close."

Yeah, no doubts on that one.

"*Cherokee*, this is Dunklin," Marcus called out. "Open your aft bay doors now and make sure to stay inside the shuttle until we come to a stop. We're coming in hot."

"Acknowledged," Yamaguchi replied.

Siobhan turned to peek back over the top of the truck, looking for gaps between legs and crates. For a moment so short it was probably a strobe's afterimage, she caught a wall of headlights in the distance. Not to the gate yet, but closing fast.

A gun on *Anna*, any gun, would have been nice, right about now. Get *Cherokee* loaded fast, since he was the lighter vehicle, then cross to *Anna*.

"Boss," Bok was suddenly in her ear. "When Markus stops moving, you need to get your ass aboard the freighter and start your preflight."

"I need to be here," she retorted. In command, as it were.

"Negative," the Boatswain snarled out the words. "We already have a partial load. If we can escape with that, we come out ahead, even if everybody else is captured. Your place is flying us home."

Siobhan ground her teeth rather than answer. He was right, of course. Bok had been doing this since before she was born, and had his shit together.

But it stung. She couldn't be *doing* anymore. She had to be *commanding*.

She turned to make eye contact through the back glass of the cab. He was all of about ten centimeters away. Apparently he had been staring at the back of her head.

"Understood," she nodded defeat.

"Ten seconds," Markus yelled. "Everybody grab on. And somebody grab Trinidad, too."

That got a round of laughs on the comm that took some of the weight off Siobhan's shoulders. She didn't have to do it all. She had a team of crazy, efficient pirates working for her.

The truck grounded hard, dragging the skids nearly a meter rather than stopping first and landing. It saved them several seconds.

And Trinidad would have gone ass over tea kettle, if he'd still been on top of the cab.

Pirates exploded into motion.

Siobhan was out the driver's door a second after Markus. She took one look at things, and then ran the fifty meters to the front door of *Anna's Vindication*, a whale's mouth intent on swallowing her whole.

Bok's two helpers were racing the other direction to help unload. They waved as they went by silently, and she was alone for the first time in a week.

Into the mouth of the beast. Across the throat. Up the gullet into the brain.

*Up the sinuses? Something.*

The bridge had not changed. Her autopilot course was still plotted. All anybody had to do was push button number one on the left side, and the ship would take itself to orbit politely enough.

But there might be incoming fire shortly.

She dialed up a link to *405* and put a map on the screen, updated as the two vehicles, big and monstrous, raced closer.

Another screen was slaved to a camera turret midship. She spun that around and watched big men and women bodily toss heavy crates to the ground, where others threw them on hand trucks and hauled them off. Even at fifty kilograms a box, the group was moving fast.

Siobhan brought the engines to ready and the repulsors just shy of lifting the vehicle, but still starting to kick up grit. *Anna* would get much heavier when the truck drove aboard, but having the collective tuned now saved her two or three seconds then.

Might make all the difference.

In the distance, the bad guys crept closer.

"*Cherokee*, you are full," Bok called over the radio. "Seal now and go for broke."

"Roger that."

On the camera, the truck began rumbling towards *Anna*, men and women running full tilt in its wake.

The shuttle's repulsors came alive and the vessel took off.

A flash of light cut the night.

"Shit," Yamaguchi yelled. "What was that?"

"You are taking ground fire from the lead vehicle, *Cherokee*," Siobhan said calmly. She hoped it sounded calm. "Begin evasive maneuvers."

The man didn't answer, but the shuttle's ascent changed chord. Grew flatter and started to wiggle.

The second shot came closer but missed. Still damned good marksmanship, especially from a moving platform at an evading target.

"Markus," Siobhan called. "Land hard when you get in and lock yourself to the deck with the magnets. We'll worry about dents in orbit. Bok, tell me when everyone is safe. Don't worry about closing the hatch first."

Both men answered.

Siobhan saw the third shot just miss clipping the shuttle.

She didn't know if they could shoot it down or not. Land vehicles were at a different scale from spaceships, but he only had to get lucky.

"All accounted for," Bok called. "Closing the bay door."

"Everyone grab something solid now," Siobhan answered, lifting the repulsor collective another notch and slamming the engine button to full thrust.

With the ship going forward, anyone not holding on would slide deeper into the ship, but that was acceptable, since the aft end was sealed off. Bruised and broken bones beat prisoner of war.

Rather than go for sky, Siobhan held the repulsors just high enough to get the ship to about fifty meters off the deck. She would never try this stunt anyplace that wasn't flat as a snooker table, but that's exactly what she had to work with here.

"Hang on," she repeated, slamming the thrusters forward so *Anna* could work up a good head of steam.

Siobhan spun the camera turret around aft and lit every external flood the ship had. She let the altitude dip to twenty meters as her velocity increased.

Overhead, that fourth shot never went at *Cherokee*, as the gunner suddenly realized she was on a ramming course with their little tank. Siobhan was close enough to see the barrel suddenly slew around and start to depress, trying to line Moby Dick up for a shot.

The mouth of the great whale finally slammed shut with an audible jolt that rang through the entire hull. Around her, Siobhan felt *Anna* speed up, without that extra parachute slowing her.

Siobhan laughed out loud with the extra, near-orgasmic surge of power from her mount, and drifted the ship to the left.

The gunner's shot went high anyway, but he also hadn't been able to track her sideslip.

Three. Two. One.

Siobhan pushed hard at the altitude controls and *Anna* stood on her ass in the moonlight, like a horse rearing up.

For the briefest moment, Siobhan was afraid she had cut it too close, as the aft of the ship pitched down as the bow when up, but there was a lot of power driving them now.

*Anna's Vindication* cleared the top of the riot control vehicle by at least five meters, near as she could tell, but that was enough.

Flying this low, this fast, and then pushing the engines into the ground had created the effect she wanted, a smoke screen of dust and dirt blasted into the air in her wake, solid enough to blind everybody, especially with every light turned on and diffusing through the cloud.

And she cleared the front end of that stupid dump truck by at least twenty meters, which was impressive, since the damned thing was at least fifty meters tall.

Siobhan wasn't too sure she couldn't have landed *Anna* on the back of the thing, if the top was flat, rather than a bowl.

But the guys on the ground stopped firing, completely blind.

Just in case, Siobhan doused all the lights suddenly and banked hard on to her side for a bit, running hard for the north pole horizon before she got much higher.

"Bok, what's the status down there?" she yelled as *Anna* finally flattened out.

"Max will be busy shortly," the Boatswain replied. "But nothing serious. Might need to shut off gravity in orbit, in order to unwedge the truck from Markus's parking job. Still better than Nakisha would have done."

"Hey!" the marine took exception. "I park better than that."

"No, you don't," Trinidad and several others weighed in as laughter filled the comm.

"*CS-405*, this is *Anna's Vindication*," Siobhan let all the mad energy flow out of her chest into her voice. "We have departed the surface. Rendezvous in orbit in three hours."

"Roger that, *Blackbeard*," Phil replied in a voice that betrayed his own relief. "Good job."

# DINNER COMPANIONS (DAY 121?
## COMMON ERA 13,449)

LAN WAS careful to keep his opinion on the topic entirely neutral, especially considering his dinner companions tonight at the small table.

Director Kosnett was charming and gracious. First Officer Lau had learned enough Mongolian to translate some alarmingly-funny jokes. The others were equally pleasant.

It was the food that concerned him. And his reaction to it, which made it much, much worse.

On the one hand, tuna had stopped being every second or third meal. Considering where this crew had gotten the tuna, Lan had originally been prepared to take umbrage at the entire affair, but these pirates could have also shot he and Kiel rather than going to the effort to feed and entertain them. There was that.

Conversely, dinner tonight was apparently a celebration. The cook had done a magnificent job with chicken, adding vegetables Lan couldn't always identify, and smothering the whole thing in an alfredo sauce that was better than Kiel could make.

Although he might never tell her that.

Lan had his suspicions as to the provenance of the meal. Some other of *Buran's* children had apparently been overwhelmed by this plague of extremely polite, mostly-friendly locusts.

Did enjoying such a repast make him an accessory after the fact to the crime of interstellar piracy? It was an interesting legalism to consider.

He supposed that some might make the case that he and his spouse should have undertaken a hunger strike rather than consume food taken from others against the common good. But that was a Warrior mentality. And the Imperials might have ignored them, letting them starve, or forcing them to eat, so nothing would have been gained.

In his heart, Lan also held firm to the belief that a Scholar would have acted thus, quietly learning as much as he could about the barbarians against the future ability to share his knowledge with others, once he was released.

Lan had no reason to doubt Director Kosnett's word. The man had been proper all this time.

Hopefully, *The Eldest* would not see fit to punish Lan as a collaborator, given the circumstances. Collaboration suggested a voluntary action, something Lan had been denied. He was a prisoner, a hostage.

All he could do at present was wait, and learn.

Next to him, as he cogitated on such deep topics, Kiel scraped the bowl clean with her spoon, getting the last bits of noodle along with the sauce.

"Chicken Alfredo?" she finally asked First Officer Lau with a grin. "Where did you steal it?"

Lan blanched at the apparently poor manners of his spouse, but then he saw the reciprocal grin on the tall woman.

*So, we are becoming fellow travelers, perhaps? Will that work to our benefit over the short term? What about the long?*

"*Barnaul*," the tall officer answered with a small laugh.

"How did you land there?" Kiel pressed on, changing languages on the fly. "I thought this ship was too large?"

Lan knew a moment of shock when he realized that both he and his spouse were learning as much Bulgarian, apparently, and becoming as comfortable in it, as the barbarians were learning the civilized tongue. He wondered if that crime would also be on their heads.

"It is," Lau said. "We used yours instead."

"Really?" Lan burst out, panicked at the thought of wanted posters with his face adorning every customs office in *The Holding*.

"It should be safe for you," Lau continued. "The crew customized the engine transponder to that of one of your competitors, according to the notes I have seen."

And yet another crime against humanity on his ledger. Lan wondered if *The Eldest* would recognize *Force majeure* as a defense, or if he and his spouse would be adjudicated guilty of *Lèse-majesté*, when it was all over.

"You assaulted the refrigerated warehouse?" Kiel asked.

She was the one who knew every planet, every culture, and every bureaucrat. Lan was just the bookkeeper on this team.

"Snuck in," Director Kosnett joined the conversation now. "My Second Officer has taken it upon herself to become a pirate. They landed, stole a flatbed, and liberated two large shipping containers and several dozen small ones before the authorities chased them off."

"Oh ho," Kiel laughed. "I would have liked to have seen the look on Beel's face when that happened. He has always been a stickler for rules, with no sense of humor. Now where are we headed, if I may ask without offering insult?"

Kosnett paused. The table paused with him. Lan realized that he and his spouse had possibly gotten too close to the heart of the matter with an innocent question. Perhaps reminded the man that they were prisoners of war, and not mere passengers.

"Normally, the path home would be to skirt *Ninagirsu*," he finally answered, surprising Lan, who had expected to be unceremoniously marched back to the cabin for their effrontery. "But, as you might expect, we think those lanes will be too heavily patrolled right now for us to sneak through. It would be less of an effort if the ship was whole, but we cannot stay in JumpSpace for weeks on end without repairs. Our jumps, as you might have noticed, are not much longer than yours would have been, on your ship."

Lan heard Kiel's quiet gasp of surprise. They had been married for more than twenty years. Others might have missed it.

Had they just been admitted to the criminal enterprise as junior members?

Kiel nodded after a shocked blip.

"For now, we are running parallel to the *M'Hanii Gulf*, looking for an area I believe will be safe enough for us to sneak through, a possum trying to cross a highway."

"First Officer Lau suggested at one point that you were using my notes on the sector, as a Gazetteer, Director Kosnett," Kiel observed neutrally.

"That is correct," Lau interjected. "We need to avoid the heavily-armed systems."

"How many more raids do you anticipate?" Kiel asked.

"Two," Kosnett said simply. "One now, and one on the far side to replenish stocks."

"I have never crossed the border frontier," Kiel said. "Trade in the Militarized Zone is tightly proscribed."

She stopped and Lan watched her eyes grow distant, squinting at something she was calculating in her head. The whole table fell silent with her, poised.

"If one drew a straight line between *Barnaul* and *Ninagirsu*, as a navigation course," she suggested carefully, "one might have taken a different path. Down forty degrees and left fifty."

Lan started almost as hard as Officer Lau did, across the table.

"Thirty-eight and forty-four," she answered after a second. "How did you know we'd go after *Laptev*?"

Kiel smiled. She glanced over at Lan. He found reassurance in that simple grin. Whatever she was up to, he would walk with her, always. Hopefully, it did not end in their execution as traitors or spies.

"It is the most isolated world facing the river of darkness," Kiel said. "Far enough from *Ninagirsu*. And a farming world, where you will be able to fill your holds with grains and vegetables frozen for transport to places like *Barnaul*. I cannot speak to the Militarized Zone."

"My notes on that side are actually much more extensive," Kosnett replied. "Nearly complete. We are a scout, leading Admiral Keller's fleet, so I have needed to maintain and update an encyclopedia of all those worlds we have explored or raided. I will send you home with some of my notes, minus only the militarily-sensitive additions."

It was Lan's turn to gasp, although Kiel joined him.

What would be that value to a merchant, of already knowing all the worlds in a new sector, were *The Eldest* to open it to trade?

Or worse, if *The Eldest* was pushed back by the dangerous warlord Keller, and perhaps the *Altai* Sector became the frontier? Would the barbarians welcome trade with civilized worlds?

Could they get rich, in what some might see as treason?

# REDNECKING (MAY 4, 402)

"WHAT AM I LOOKING AT?" Siobhan asked, standing in the hatchway to the machine shop, studying the *thing* Markus Dunklin was holding in two hands.

It looked vaguely like a pulse rifle. Bastard cousin, maybe. Pistol grips front and back. All black. But the barrel looked big enough for her to put a fist down it.

Trinidad was hovering over her shoulder as they watched, but he hadn't said anything yet. Just breathing quietly on her.

"So Nakisha wanted a bigger boom," Markus said defensively.

Nakisha *always* wanted a bigger boom. That girl was a little unbalanced, even for a marine.

"Uh huh," Siobhan grunted ambiguously.

That was the problem with motivated folks. Occasionally they went sideways on you. She had no idea what was up, other than Markus asking her and Trinidad to come down to the machine shop to see something.

"Had an idea the other day," Markus continued, holding his new prize up for them to look at.

"What does it do?" Siobhan prodded the man.

"Oh," he said, surprised. "Right. It's a rocket launcher."

"A what?" Trinidad asked.

His tone was even more unbelieving.

"I looked up arrows," Markus said, going utterly sideways on them. "Works kinda like a crossbow."

"Back up," Siobhan stopped him cold. "Why did you build a rocket launcher?"

"Well, because I don't have the parts to build a pulse cannon," he answered.

Siobhan counted the three in her head. She *had* phrased her question badly. He had answered it. She was willing to give her favorite crazy redneck that. It probably made perfect sense to him.

"Why do we *need* a rocket launcher, perhaps?" she corrected herself.

"Oh, right," he repeated himself. Must be a nervous twitch. She had known enough engineers to see that. "So we might have gotten into trouble, back on the mining world. Pulse rifle won't kill anything with any amount of armor. Figure that riot control truck would have just laughed at us. And we couldn't get close enough to roll a grenade under him, like we did the police car. Plus the dirt wouldn't have been as effective to shape the explosion upward."

"Okay, I'm with you so far," Siobhan admitted. Had those cops been on the ball faster, over at the mine, then they might not have made it off of *Barnaul* at all. "Continue."

"We got grenades," Markus said. "Crates of them, according to Nakisha and Gerry, over on *405*. Had an idea about how to deliver them. Haven't tested it yet, but the theory works."

Thank the Creator he hadn't tested it. The ship was already crowded, even with both of those big shipping containers moved over to the mothership, since the flatbed truck stayed here.

"Tell me the theory, Dunklin," Trinidad spoke up.

"So I got a tube," the engineer said. "Machined it clean and then added a single spiral of rifling. That's steel. Machined another tube of steel, smaller, and then coated it over with a thin layer of lead, so I could cam it into place like a bullet and hold it when the fuel ignited."

"Fuel?" Siobhan asked, concerned where this boy was headed.

"Yeah," Markus's whole face lit up with a smile. "That was the genius idea. Lined the inner tube with a layer of solid combustible. That's the rocket fuel. But the back bit is a different mix. It'll burn a little slower, and a lot cooler. Just enough oomph to get the rocket out of the barrel, and spinning slightly for stability, when the burn-through hits the hot stuff and it goes zip. Well, crack, technically."

"Technically?" Siobhan wondered if she had wandered into an intellectual desert and gotten lost.

"Breaking the sound barrier, boss," Markus said helpfully. "We're subsonic in the barrel, so lower pressure. Once clear, we can go faster. On the front, I machined some cradles to hold standard grenades. You arm it when you put the rocket in the barrel, and then it will explode on impact. Just don't try to shoot through trees or something."

"Okay," Trinidad said. "I'm not a rocket physicist, even if I did play one in a vid. Who did the math on all this?"

"I did," Markus replied. "Nothing more complex than some orbital geometry stuff, plus a lot of pressure modeling for the metallurgy. Got it all saved in the computer for Bok to review at some point."

Siobhan made a note to send that file to Bok the *very next time* the two ships were within communication range of each other, and long before they needed to use Dunklin's new toy.

"And Nakisha can kill a riot patrol vehicle with it?" Trinidad asked.

"Should," Markus smiled a kilometer wide. "She gave me the specs for the model she used to drive when she was Shore Patrol. Pretty sure a direct hit will shatter a decent-sized hole in the side. Lower and you can break an axle, if it has wheels, or put all sorts of shrapnel into the repulsors, which is just as good."

"And we need this…why?" Siobhan asked.

"We're pirates," Markus pronounced, as if it was obvious and she was a little too dense to see that.

"And you need to test this on a planetary surface?" she continued. Emphasis on *you*, since there was no way in hell she was going to be anywhere near it. Let Markus and Nakisha take those risks.

"Don't need atmosphere," Markus noted. "Just a surface *g* of at least forty percent, so we can approximate flight dynamics. *405*'s got the sensors for that."

"And it will take smoke grenades?" Trinidad asked.

"Uhm, probably," Markus's face fell into so much confusion that Siobhan nearly laughed out loud.

Trust the redneck to worry about blowing things up, rather than just hiding from bad guys.

They were pirates, after all.

# COUNCIL OF WAR (MAY 11, 402)

How MANY TIMES had he sat on that side of the conversation and watched Keller do this? Phil couldn't really count, unless every big raid or event counted. He had that number in his head.

Motivate the troops, but not by appealing to their patriotic nature. After all, they carried the flag of the *Fribourg Empire*, these days. A few of the others even wore the uniform, although Phil couldn't ever see himself going down that path.

No, Keller had always made her point in light of some greater mission. He had even gone back and viewed some of the operational logs from events with the old, inner circle, back when it was just her with Denis Jež, Alber' d'Maine, and Tomas Kigali. Even Robbie Aeliaes had only come along later, although he had known Jessica from before, when she commanded *Brightoak* and he was part of her squadron.

Greater cause. In those early days, starting a psychological war with *Fribourg* on a normally quiet border, the place where tertiary fleets patrolled just enough to keep pirates and smugglers at bay, but never challenged the big gap between nations. Until Keller came along.

Rather like *M'Hanii*.

Jessica would appeal to this group in the light of saving galactic humanity from being taken under the heel of a deathless machine intent on becoming a god.

But Jessica wasn't here today. First Expeditionary Fleet had hopefully made the right assumption that something had gone wrong, and that they needed to vanish into the night. One captured corvette was a tragedy. Losing First Expeditionary would have been a catastrophe. He and his people were forlorn, at this point.

As they should be.

Phil looked down the conference table at his team. It wasn't much, as councils of war went, but it was all he had. Heather, Kam, Evan, and Bok from the main crew. Trinidad and Siobhan, who he had taken to thinking of as *Lady Blackbeard*, from the prize.

The conference room felt fuller than it was, but that was the outsized personalities involved. The sense of mission and confidence that they *were* making a difference here.

That much, he could promise to Keller as success on his part, as they made their way home. He had already done damage to *Buran*'s economy, however small it was, by capturing *Resolute Revolution*, and by the raid on *Barnaul*.

But the psychological impact had to be much greater. Keller had never actively captured freighters, only destroying a few at places like *Yenisei* and *Stanovoy*. And she had never set troops down on a planetary surface, after that very first raid, even before *Trusski*, when she wanted to anchor a line of retreat.

Phil Kosnett had upped the ante with *Buran*. Planetary constabularies would be clamoring for defensive forces, this far behind the nominal lines. More ships. More missiles.

More troops. And those would have to come from somewhere. More importantly, word would get out.

But it wasn't going to be enough, and he knew that. They were going to need to do more. Get meaner, and start punching well above their weight category. This was a warship of the *Republic of Aquitaine* Navy, by the gods.

Keller had told them that her mission was to make the people of *The Holding* fear her more than they did their overlord. If the *Lord of Winter* started to look weak, how many worlds would panic?

The faces had grown expectant, in Phil's moments of introspection. Calm, but with a layer of anger just under the surface. Poised.

Nobody would forget *St. Legier*. What it meant to Centurion Wiegand. What *The Eldest* had done to the galaxy. He needed to tap that rage now.

"I had considered the need to load up *Queen Anne's Revenge* with as much food as it would hold," Phil suddenly began, the conversations in his head taking shape to include his commanders as his eyes lit on Siobhan Skokomish. *Lady Blackbeard.* "Sending you home as fast as you could run, to make arrangements for a supply ship to get us parts and food out here, while we hid in a safe, quiet place."

Phil placed both hands flat on the surface of the table as the others began to lean in. He wasn't a dominating, charismatic speaker. Not like Keller. But he could make an effective point verbally when he needed to. Like now.

"But we're in the middle of a war zone out here, people," he continued. "We already know what the defenses are like, across the Gulf, and, thanks to Kiel's notes, we have a pretty good idea what we'll face over here, at least until those folks start shifting in bigger fleets to stop us and Keller from raiding at will."

He paused for a moment, scanning every face.

Yes, they were in, whatever it was. They would be there with him.

"Keller always believed that *Buran's* fleet is actually not that much larger than *Fribourg's*, counting vessels," he said. "Their different technology and tactics made them more effective, at least until we came along with Expeditionary classes. The Corvette/Scout design is the weakest line warship in the fleet, right now. That's us. We can't charge in and blow things up, like a Heavy Dreadnaught can, so we have to be sneaky. And with a crew of just over two hundred souls, it's not like we can capture a planet, or even hold a station for long."

Nods now. His people, used to the way he thought. Phil Kosnett, Explorer. Rather than Phil Kosnett, Berserker-At-Arms. He was no Tom Kigali.

But he was still a sailor in the *Republic of Aquitaine* Navy. It was time they remembered what that meant.

"I had considered sneaking us all home and calling it good," he observed. "Certainly, that would have been enough, to fulfill our standing orders, especially with the raids we would need to do on the way, just to keep eating and stay away from the oatmeal."

Chuckles. Faces turning to Siobhan. *Blackbeard's* normally dark face actually showing a blush, something Phil wasn't sure he had ever seen before.

"We're not doing that," Phil dropped his first bombshell.

"We're not?" Heather managed to speak over the sudden noise from everyone.

"No," Phil said, eyes boring in on Siobhan's. "We're going to take the war to *Buran* and do as much damage as we can, here and now. Keller will have to move *Forward Base Omicron*, since she can't take the risk that we were captured and might reveal its location. That will take her offline for a while, which can't be helped. I have no intention of letting *Buran* have the time to relax and recover."

"So after *Laptev*?" Siobhan's voice managed to be both quiet and fierce at the same time. Her eyes seemed to be filled with a black plasma that glowed, even as dark as they were.

"I want to know how much food we can steal at *Laptev*," Phil said. "That's our limiting factor right now, since the JumpSails are about as good as they can get without us taking the ship apart in a drydock. Even with improvised fixed, Bok thinks we have a handle on them. At least enough of one. How long can we stay out here, blowing things up and setting minds on fire, while Keller recovers?"

"Second front?" Heather asked.

Phil laughed.

"If there were warships I could somehow steal, then, yes," he replied. "But no freighters are armed, and *Buran's* warships are all *Sentient*. But very few systems are truly defended, right now, on this side of the frontier. How many of those little, automated stations can we rob or destroy? How much panic can we induce, with one Corvette/Scout and an attitude problem?"

"You're forgetting *Anna's Vindication*," Siobhan barked.

"No more than I would Odysseus's Horse, Skokomish," Phil replied. "I want you to take down the walls of Troy for me."

Her eyes got the look Phil was waiting for. Distant, angry, contemplative. She nodded.

No words were necessary. He had them now.

It was time for them to start a second front in *Keller's War*.

# DWARF GIANT (MAY 27, 402)

As always in these situations, Phil put himself on the Main Bridge, with Heather forward in the Emergency Bridge. The big change today was that he had rotated Evan Brinich forward, so that Heather had the Science Officer with her in the same space, instead of just on the comm.

This was a combat setting. She had Tactical command and would need every edge she could get.

In the past, *CS-405* had been the third choice for scouting. At least in Keller's mind. But then, she had the Galactic Survey Cruiser *Ballard*, with some of the best folks in the business, plus *CP-406*, a dedicated scout/raider with portable firepower far in excess of the smaller Corvette/Scout. They could sneak, scout, AND shoot.

*405*'s job had been to protect the inner squadron while Keller sent the other two out to do things. His mission had been defensive, always. Blinding their enemies while sailing in the line ahead of *Vanguard*, and before that, *Auberon*. Taking shots at targets of opportunity with his short-range beams, while the other girls and boys tangled with the big enemies.

Today, it was their mission to do the long-range scouting for the rest of the team.

They were exactly backwards to the normal approach, as Phil checked his screens. *Anna's Vindication* was a few light years away, quietly waiting in the darkness for them to return, while Heather and her team sidled into the *Laptev* system and scouted it for a raid.

"All hands, prepare to transition to JumpSpace," Heather's voice filled the bridge as Phil watched. "Phase Two complete."

So far, so good.

*Laptev*'s stellar parent was about as boring as they went: an orange Mainstream at the dwarf end of things, just warm enough to have a broad habitable zone for colonization, but generally throwing out a lesser solar wind than many of the yellower stars. Phil presumed it was an older generation of star, and thus middle-aged.

One world with a population, centered almost exactly in the habitable zone.

Closer in to the star was a cinder of a planet where lead ran liquid on the surface and the core had long since cooled to solid iron. Farther out, another dead world, this one more black from surface layers of carbon, that never had enough oxygen to be worth terraforming.

Their next drop-out into RealSpace would put the ship into close orbit of a dwarf gas giant, a world just barely large enough to have retained that depth of atmosphere, without the solar wind stripping it off. Interestingly, at least to the explorer in his soul, this world was largely red, having gotten most of the iron that should have been part of a rockier world closer in.

He wondered what had happened to disturb the early solar system here, but was glad it had. The dwarf giant was noted for having sixteen moons of various sizes and inclinations, with most of them comprised almost exclusively of base iron, one of the most common materials a stellar technology had access to.

And thus, nothing worth even maintaining a simple mining outpost here. That was good. No reason to even be in the vicinity.

Phil checked his boards. Bok had figured out just how much stress the secondary JumpSail could take before the matrix started to feed on itself and overheat. They didn't have the tools or materials to hold it together when it did, but they could plan their jumps by the number of minutes they had, under normal circumstances, before they needed to shut it down and let it cool while they reset the controllers.

Nothing about today, hopefully, would be pushing that envelope.

"Stand by for emergence," Heather called to the crew. "All gun crews, you are unlocked for possible combat."

Better to try to kill something if they managed to stumble into a bad situation right now, than to spend precious moments letting another ship get away and warn the redcoats.

With Siobhan's team elsewhere, there were no friendly vessels local. Just risk and complications.

*Emergence.* Back on the blind side of the planet, seen from the perspective of *Laptev*'s orbit. And far enough away that nobody would see you, as long as you were quiet.

Clear sailing awaited them. Nothing on the sensors but moons.

Time to get to work.

"All gun teams, you are now locked," Heather said over the line. "Remain on standby for emergency action, if necessary."

There was a technique to being a scout in hostile territory. Phil missed having Siobhan here, right now, as she had an absolute flair for maneuvering, but West would do good enough.

This job called for patience, above everything. West had that, in spades.

"Stand by to broach," Heather walked forward with the process.

From here, they would be just another moon, only partially visible on the far side of the dwarf giant, and then only if someone locked on the area with active sensors, which would make them stand out against the darkness and warn *405*. Even on optical cameras, the dwarf's atmosphere was too rough for this ship to get any attention as they suddenly appeared around a horizon.

Main Bridge was keyed up, since West was still here, rather than up front, but they were all virtually in the same room right now.

"Pilot, execute your broach," came the order.

Phil wasn't mirroring Evan's boards. That would be overwhelming right now, with the amount of data the scout would be gathering.

Unlike the Galactic Survey Cruisers, the Corvette/Scout had sensor arrays at both ends of the vessel, where other corvettes had their Type-3 beams installations. These were as good as *Ballard*'s, but having them that far apart meant that Evan could also get an amazing parallax on a target, even at eight AU from the star, just over one light hour, and roughly the same distance to *Laptev*, currently coming up on the dwarf giant's orbit from behind.

No, Phil wanted to see what was out there. Or rather, who.

Kiel had fantastic notes on the planetary culture and bureaucratic tides, but the possible defenses were a blank spot. Something she took for granted.

Plus, she and Lan had only been here a few times, since

the planet tended to import and export in massive bulk, rather than small, specialist transports like *Anna's Vindication*.

Phil watched Evan's sensors assemble an image of *Laptev's* orbital occupants.

There, the station. Larger than the little, automated ones around most worlds, since *Laptev* had a significantly-large interstellar economy, compared to many of *Buran's* worlds in this sector. Phil assumed it had some level of firepower, since they had run into a similar platform at *Yenisei*. Probably heavy cruiser-levels of firepower or better, if he was dumb enough to get into a duel with it. Those folks would eat his lunch.

Briefly, idly, he wondered if they could program the autopilot on *Anna's Vindication* to simply ram the station and blow itself up, possibly destroying the station in the process.

Not worth the other troubles, since that ship was the only Trojan Horse he had right now, but worth considering, if he was serious about taking up destructive piracy as a vocation.

Something didn't look right in the image. Phil puzzled at it for several seconds, until finally Evan's sensors gathered enough data to resolve the visuals better. He had probably run into the same question himself, and tweaked things.

The thing they were seeing was a stock design, after all. *Buran* was all about standards for things. Mass standardization whenever possible. What had thrown everything off was that docked with the station was a ship that was larger than *CS-405*. Hell, that thing was bigger than the Heavy Dreadnaught *Vanguard*. Maybe approaching a Star Controller, for scale.

Quickly, Phil flipped to the Imperial recognition file, augmented significantly after the raids at *Stanovoy* and *Yenisei*.

There. Oh, my.

"Evan, confirm the signal I've highlighted," Phil ordered over the line, sending an image from the file forward to the Emergency Bridge.

Heather was in tactical command right now, but it was Phil's boat.

And Phil's mission.

"Confirmed, Commander," Evan replied after a few moments. "Trying to read his signals with the station now. They're encrypted, but it's not a military-grade cypher. Should be able to punch through it in a bit."

"Keep me posted, EmBridge," Phil said. "This changes things significantly for us."

"What's on your mind, Phil?" Heather asked.

He could hear the careful tones, like she knew he was up to even worse no-good than normal.

"You're going to join Siobhan on this one, Heather," he replied.

There was a pause.

"Think we can do it?" she pressed.

"*Blackbeard* and Trinidad will see it as a challenge, Tactical," he smiled. It felt like a shark's smile.

"Roger that," Heather said. "Stand by to dive."

Back down behind the shield of the planet, so they could turn and run for deep space.

Things were about to get thrilling.

And perilous.

# ODYSSEUS (JUNE 1, 402)

SIOBHAN REMEMBERED to shut her mouth when it fell open in shock.

Eventually.

The thing Evan was projecting on the conference room screen was huge. As starships went, it was the biggest civilian vessel she had ever encountered. *Aquitaine* went in for smaller ships, running on more efficient direct spokes, as a rule, rather than using an older, railroad model, where you flew a fixed pattern of systems. *Fribourg* trade networks never really even got that big, working within a culture that believed in righteous self-sufficiency for most planets.

But *Buran* was all about eking out the maximum efficiency at the minimum cost. Whenever, wherever, however it needed to do that. It probably helped that they weren't all that into free trade, at least when official policy favored something one of her instructors had once classified as industrialism.

No, *Buran* commanded the heights, and ran its economy that way. Little people, like Kiel and Lan, made do at the margins, bringing in specialty goods that were a rare treat, and could make a good living at it, but they would never be an economic threat.

Because that monster over there could haul gigatons of freight, world to world, working on planetary scales and budgets.

Wow.

As Evan worked, he brought up a second image beside the first, this one from the standard recognition file. Sure enough. Big monster. A bit under two kilometers, from bow to stern, but lacking any of the elegance of a warship. Just as an efficient a use of volume as physically possible.

Honestly, it looked like a stick of butter with a stack of engines tacked onto the end.

"Because *Buran*'s warships look vaguely like terrestrial sharks, we believe that is the reason *The Holding* names them thus," Evan was saying. "But nobody has ever encountered one of these beasts in its native habitat, nor gotten close enough to capture one. They only run on this side of the *M'Hanii Gulf*. For our notes, we've classified it as a humpback whale. Big and slow, krill feeder, rather than predator, but not the biggest possible cetacean. There is a larger size of freight-hauling vessel, almost a mobile station, that *Fribourg* calls a Blue Whale class."

"So how do we know this intel?" Siobhan felt her hand go up. The bright kid with the annoying questions in the orbital dynamic class.

"*Fribourg* has a few spies," Phil replied instead. "And Keller's tame defector has been happily filling in details. This he did back when he hoped trade would settle the border disputes."

"So those numbers are believable?" she continued. "Total crew of only about thirty people on a ship *Auberon*'s size?"

"You'd be amazed, how much of that volume is pure cargo, Siobhan," Evan said, clicking something to shift to a schematic drawing and lighting various areas up. "The engines are all of this section, just to push against that much mass and get it moving. The control tower is here with living spaces above. The spine runs all the way forward, but all it does is define an area. Those two big containers you stole at *Barnaul*? Things like those go two-deep, end to end, in silos inserted into the belly, twelve to a row-width, and something like one hundred rows long. Fully loaded, we're looking at something in the neighborhood of two hundred and forty silos by count, but many of the boxes here are much larger instead, taking up a full depth, by four spaces on each side."

"How the hell do you move them around?" Siobhan heard herself ask.

"Specialized freighters like *Anna's Vindication*, give or take," Heather replied. "Cargo tugs like *CT-9492*, that hauls the parts of our mobile base. In this case, they can transport something like four of the big pods between ground and sky."

"And you want to steal this thing?" Siobhan turned to Phil.

She hadn't believed him then. Still wasn't sure she did now. As piracy went, this was off the charts-crazy.

And right up her alley, if she had to admit it in public, which she probably would, with this group.

"You and Heather," Phil answered. "And *Queen Anne's Revenge*."

"What about the station?" Siobhan pursued. "Thing's armed."

"I want you to think about how you would do it," Phil smiled at her like a shark.

She grinned back. Let her mind wander a bit.

Considered Trinidad and Nakisha, making a pirate vid. All the myriad, silly ways they might bluff their way in, scramble door codes, cut airlock hatches. The lies they would have to come up with.

She nodded to Phil and felt the grin broaden into a smile.

"Can't be done," she said simply. "We haven't got the bodies or firepower to raid a station like that and get away safe. Certainly not to steal a ship like that from under their noses."

Faces fell around her as she dashed their hopes. That ship represented a massive amount of food. Perhaps as much as two years without a single bit of rationing. Never again oatmeal. And that was not taking into account the value of the hull itself, or the disruption of trade that would result from taking it out of the line.

Siobhan felt her own evil angels start a merry pirate's chorus in her head. It was a good thing she was an officer and a gentlewoman, and not a full-time buccaneer, because she might get pretty good at this.

Briefly, she considered her Plan B, which was to just hammer the damned thing to rubble with the Type-1-Pulse beams, setting the generators to run hot and then woodpeckering the bastard.

But that was nowhere near as much fun as Plan A.

"However," Siobhan continued before anyone got too sad, "there is a much easier way to do this. You all have been approaching this like a military target. That's just all levels of wrong."

"How should we be thinking?" Heather asked, face scrunched up.

Siobhan liked Heather. Respected her as a damned good officer who would be a great commander, one of these years.

If anything, the woman was a little too spit-and-polish for this sort of thing. They could fix that.

"First, we'll need to turn you into a proper pirate," Siobhan smirked.

# IN WAIT (JUNE 4, 402)

HEATHER FELT LIKE AN OUTSIDER HERE, but that was only natural. Siobhan and her team had been in residence in *Anna's Vindication* for two months now, which was enough time to begin to personalize things.

Like the shipping label for a crate of berries, apparently stolen as part of the raid on *Barnaul*, and now attached to the front bulkhead of the bridge, a little below the view port. Above it, a picture of a tuna had been stuck to the wall as well, so possibly Heather was seeing the beginnings of a totem pole, or at least a visual chain of raids.

She was in the left-hand seat today. Heather could fly the little freighter from here, but Siobhan was handling that from the right. Aft, all of the original raiders were waiting in suits, plus an extra group of engineers who Bok considered safe enough with prybars to not hurt anyone accidentally.

It felt odd, not being in uniform. According to regulations, they all should have been in full uniforms when performing this mission, so that they would be treated as prisoners of war, rather than pirates, if something went wrong and they were captured, but *The Holding* had never established formal, diplomatic ties to *Fribourg* or *Aquitaine*, so the Laws of War were not officially in practice.

Keller had just enforced them anyway, at *Trusski*.

But being in civilian gear, according to Siobhan, would get Heather into the right mindset to become a swashbuckler, whatever that meant. The lifesuits they would wear for EVA were standard fleet issue, so there would be no doubt that Heather belonged to an organized military force. It was just the clothing underneath.

Still, it felt odd. It tugged odd, and wrinkled strangely, compared to her uniform. Maybe that was the whole point.

Siobhan's people rarely called the woman by her name, Heather had noted. Instead, *Lady Blackbeard,* or some variant of it, seemed to be the preferred nomenclature. And Trinidad Mildon had become *Stunt Dude,* which made no sense at all to Heather, but invariably generated giggles within that group.

Heather wondered if she would need a pirate nickname, before this was all done. And what that might entail. While she was technically the senior officer present, Phil had impressed upon her that Siobhan was command centurion on the raider *Anna's Vindication,* what everyone had gone back to calling *Queen Anne's Revenge* in private, however brevet Siobhan's rank might be. It was her ship.

And, if they managed to take the other one, Heather would brevet as well, commanding a freighter large enough to have multiple telecomm codes.

"Whachathinkin'?" Siobhan glanced over and grinned.

They had time to kill. It had taken another three days, before that humpback had announced that it was ready to depart, *CS-405* having snuck in to hide behind Phil's Dwarf Giant and watch.

"Honestly?" Heather replied to Siobhan's nod. "Pirate fashion."

"Indeed?" Siobhan's dark face lit up with a grin. "Good."

"You want me to think like a bandit, and not an officer?" Heather asked.

"That's the plan, Heather," Siobhan said. "Keller said she wanted to drive that computer god nuts with craziness. Can you think of a crazier thing than pirates suddenly running roughshod over the daisies in the back yard?"

Heather didn't have to force the chuckle. She could see the change that had come over the younger woman since Phil unleashed her on an unsuspecting galaxy.

"Just nervous," Heather admitted. "I've only ever commanded from a deck. Never taken part in a boarding action or such. This will be a new thing for me."

"You'll do fine," Siobhan reassured her. "Most of what I have to do is sit back and answer whatever strategic questions come from *Stunt Dude* or Bok, and then let their people handle things. You'll be in the same position."

"And if we screw up?" Heather asked. "Then what?"

"Then we're put in a prison," Siobhan shrugged. "Or hung from the highest yardarm. Nobody really knows, because *Buran* had never wanted to trade back for prisoners. Until *Stanovoy*, nobody had ever captured a warship intact to even take some."

"So what about *Fribourg* prisoners?" Heather wondered. "They just disappear?"

"Don't know," Siobhan said. "Not in anything I've read or heard about."

"Make a note," Heather ordered, her background coming to the fore. "We need intelligence on those people. What happens to a ship that *Buran* captures, at someplace like *Samara*?"

"Will do, boss," Siobhan lapsed into Second Officer to Heather's First, for just a moment, before *Lady Blackbeard* smiled through. "Maybe we'll need to convince Phil to raid a government office on some remote planet, sometime after this, so we can steal all their records and look it up. Emperor Karl VIII would probably reward us pretty good."

"We're military officers, Siobhan," Heather chided lightly. "We're not supposed to be doing this for the money."

"And that's where I need to work on you some more, Heather," *Lady Blackbeard* replied. "We're pirates, and we need to think like it. Officers are predictable. Pirates are black swan events that just mess everything up. Ruin everybody's day."

"I shall take that under advisement," Heather said with a laugh.

Maybe she could be a bandit, after all. *Lady Blackbeard* would be a pretty good teacher.

A light on the console between them cut the conversation.

"Here we go," Siobhan said.

She opened the PA system to bring the two dozen other crew up to date.

"Message from *CS-405*," *Blackbeard* announced in a voice Heather could only quantify as *hungry*. "*Humpback-1* has backed away from the station and aligned itself for the next stage on his road. Kosnett confirms that they will be headed to *Kamchatka* next, and taking three hops to get to their system departure. All hands to battle stations. Prepare for our first jump across."

Because Siobhan was commanding, Heather had been the one to plot the jump coordinates.

It was weird, dealing with a civilian mindset. Because they had to follow a fixed pattern of stops, a sequence apparently being flown by several vessels like this simultaneously, *Humpback-1* was in no hurry to get somewhere. Rigidity of schedule was more important that speed, apparently.

From *Laptev* orbit, the first jump was straight up, relative to the plane of the other planets, just to get clear of the thicker disk of materials at the solar equator. Then a jump exactly across the system, like staying on a valence shell, so that they would be exactly above the spot in *Laptev*'s orbit where the planet would be in roughly eleven months, or half a circle. The third jump would take the great whale to the edge of the heliosphere, and only then would it head into deep space.

But that gave *Queen Anne's Revenge* a head start. And that was what all pirates really wanted.

"All set," Heather announced quietly, confirming the flight path and gravity lines.

"Why don't you trigger it, Heather," *Blackbeard* seemed to growl back. "You'll need the practice."

Heather shared a grim grin, feeling a new doorway in her career open before her. One she had never imagined.

She pressed the button, and *Queen Anne's Revenge* twisted sideways into JumpSpace.

*I have become a buccaneer.*

# THE STALK (JUNE 5, 402)

THE FIRST JUMP had gone well. Siobhan had even gotten lucky with the second, drifting Heather's target zone just a wee bit as she first lined it up. Something about the local hydrogen density had suggested she come in a little shorter than planned, before shutting down all the external systems and going as dark as they could.

Little things that went into being a bad-ass pirate babe.

That damned whale had come out less than six light minutes away, almost directly in front of them. Pinged the vicinity with a searchlight that let everyone know where he was, and who.

Hopefully, *Anna* had appeared to be just another ugly lump of iron in the distance. Certainly, Siobhan's electronic eyes would have resolved the whale as nothing more than an asteroid at this distance, even after Evan and Bok had done so much work to tune them better. *Anna* was still a civilian freighter, like the other. The whale might not even notice they were here.

Still, nothing moving on a dangerous vector. Nobody

close that might represent a threat. Just little old us, hiding over here in the bushes.

Siobhan turned to Heather, patiently waiting in the co-pilot seat.

"If they follow form, it will take them a minimum of three more hours until they're ready for the next jump," Siobhan said. "That's why we could nap in between things here. Now it gets exciting."

"You have a fascinating definition of excitement, *Blackbeard*," Heather replied with a smile that showed just how nervous the woman really was. "Sometimes I wish we could have done this from *405*, instead of *Anna*."

"Yeah, but there was no way to be sneaky about *CS-405*," Siobhan answered. "Here, we've got crazier options."

"I'm glad you phrased it that way," Heather's laugh still had a touch of hysteria under it, but she was getting better. More grounded. "I'm not sure I would have thought to try something this insane. This desperate."

"We'll make you a pirate yet, lady," Siobhan smiled.

Now, time to get completely insane, by any standards you wanted to measure.

"All hands," Siobhan keyed the mic. "Stand by for the assault jump. Gimme green lights everywhere before I commit, because there's no backing out at that point."

She watched Heather take a moment to check her lifesuit, including the pistol on her hip. A moment later, the Senior Centurion picked up her helmet and locked it down, faceplate still open so she could talk, but all set for walking in space. A green light appeared as Heather pushed the button to check in.

Siobhan did the same, just to double check. She stretched all fingers and made fists, imagining Trinidad checking his gun for the eighth or eleventh time. That brought a smile to her face.

Across the board, twenty more lights went green.

"*Stunt Dude*," Siobhan said. "I show everyone ready."

"Affirmative, *Blackbeard*," her stunt man sidekick replied.

Siobhan reached up and latched her helmet shut. The internal systems kicked in and pressurized. Heather joined her a second later.

She was on the internal comm now.

Keller wants crazy? Top this.

"All hands, prepare for death pressure," Siobhan ordered over the private channel. "Bok, you are clear to open us to deep space."

Red lights came on everywhere as *Anna* grew nervous around them. They were in the depths of space, and someone was telling the ship to suck all the air out of the corridors. She wanted everyone warned that bad things were coming.

On Siobhan's helmet's HUD, the pressure began to drop, and her suit stiffened ever so slightly. She confirmed the course she had plotted, and that her suit had a good communications link to the ship's piloting system.

She nodded to Heather, pivoted her seat, and rose. Heather was a step behind her down the stairs, and then down to the cargo level.

Technically, one of them was supposed to remain behind on the bridge in order to pilot *Anna*, but Siobhan didn't want to be left behind on what she thought of as her mission, and Heather needed to be there, learning the ropes.

And what was Phil going to do? Court Martial them for acting like pirates?

She laughed to herself.

"What's so funny?" Heather asked.

"What Phil's going to say when he finds out," Siobhan replied.

"We are the officers on the scene," Heather quoted

primly. "We need operational authority to meet situational requirements."

"That sounds so much better than *making this shit up as we go*," Siobhan laughed again.

"I agree," Heather joined her.

The front bay door on the cargo deck was down, a ramp into infinity, or the mouth of a killer whale sneaking up on a humpback to take a bite. The target was invisible at this distance, but Siobhan could see him in her mind's eye.

*Right there, just waiting for us, basking in the solar wind.*

Bok greeted them at the bottom of the stairs. Handed them each a grapple line to latch themselves onto the side of the bay.

You were not supposed to be open to deep space while in Jump. The theory said that if you passed outside of the envelope of the Jump matrix, you should just drop back into RealSpace at the mathematical point that matched the JumpSpace coordinates.

Siobhan didn't feel like testing the theory out today, so everybody had a physical attachment, hooked at both ends, so they couldn't somehow go out that door into eternity.

Bok touched faceplates with her when she was latched. Heather was as well.

"Ready to go," he said.

Siobhan pulled out a small tablet computer and triple-checked that she could talk to the bridge. All good.

She braced herself, facing forward into the black depths. Glanced around to see Heather matching her posture.

*Humpback-1*was six light minutes away, more or less at rest, relative to *Anna*. They would be in JumpSpace for less than two seconds.

Siobhan nodded and pressed the jump button.

Black space turned to a mottled, gray, like a badly-tuned vid channel picking up cross-interference.

It was gone so fast that she might have imagined it, but over the last two months, Siobhan had spent a lot of time on the bridge, staring out into the infinite void that existed between universes. Something she never did aboard *CS-405*. Nobody did.

It was her friend now. Or at least, not as inimical an enemy.

*And there he is.*

Siobhan grinned fiercely at the outcome of her jump. She had programmed the coordinates she wanted, and then set the grav-sensors to home in on any dimple. A ship that big had enough mass to warp space-time, just the slightest bit, if you put the sensors on paranoid.

He was less than a kilometer away, at about a forty degree angle, more or less at rest.

Siobhan turned to the crew of pirates who would be accompanying her, including the newest pirate in their ranks, Senior Centurion Heather Lau.

"Radio silence from here," she said simply. "See you on the other side."

Siobhan unlatched the grapple from the ship and tucked it into her belt. They could always use them over there to stay attached to the enemy hull.

She took three, running steps and threw herself into space like a diver entering water.

Backpack thrusters came live with compressed gas, pushing her hard forward, towards the Spanish fort her crew needed to capture.

*Blackbeard's coming.*

# BUCCANEER (JUNE 5, 402)

HEATHER WATCHED Siobhan jump into her destiny with both feet, like a kid with a fresh mud puddle. It set a good example. Jarred Heather's mind loose from wanting to stop and think about how crazy this was, or reconsider a better approach angle.

They were in the chute now, no going back.

Heather's training surged to the fore and drove her after *Lady Blackbeard*. Into the cold, lonely depths of space.

Around her, the other twenty pirates on this suicide mission followed, riding forward on compressed gases and their own craziness.

In the screen slaved to a rearward view, Heather watched *Anna's Vindication* wink out of existence, like a soap bubble. She had been physically present for all of about eight seconds, and now was bouncing out to her next stop, where Phil could find the vessel, waiting patiently empty if all this failed.

Hopefully, the ship over there hadn't noticed the brief aberration on her flank. Or, if she had, it had been gone again so fast that they would log it as a sensor failure and nothing more.

Who would bip into RealSpace just long enough to throw a boarding party at an enemy ship, and then disappear?

Crazy-ass pirates, like her.

Heather wondered if Keller's folks, her other people back in *Corynthe*, ever did something like this. Or perhaps they would add it to their repertoire after this, unwilling to be upstaged by the *RAN*.

She laughed in the confines of her own, little world.

And just like that, twenty-two little guppies came to rest near the side of the humpback whale. This wasn't a ship anymore. It was a wall, a station in deep space, but they should all be inside of a Jump envelope now, if the locals panicked and triggered a jump early.

Just in case, Heather joined Trinidad in attaching her line to the side of the ship, not far from what appeared to be a ventral airlock, a bit forward from the engines.

Radio silence. Just her and her morbid thoughts about how insane this plan was. To steal a freighter by secretly boarding it in deep space, between jumps. One for the record books, most likely.

Now, the truly dangerous part started.

This was an enemy vessel. Damaging or capturing it would materially impact the economy of this sector. They kept repeating that mantra. The folks aboard were all civilians, rather than professional warriors, but they were between Heather and the success of her mission.

And time was more important than pretty.

Bok was recognizable by his bulk and compact frame. Heather wasn't sure who the other engineer that went into the airlock with him was. Trinidad was the third, in case the people up on the bridge woke up suddenly and were able to react fast enough.

Highly unlikely, but you have to assume competence on the part of the other guy, and then work against that. Of course, there wasn't much those folks could do at this point.

Even jumping blind would just prevent *CS-405* from coming to the pirates' aid. It wouldn't stop Siobhan or Heather.

Three bodies piled back out of the airlock quickly, pivoting around helpful hands held out to swing them clear.

Heather was across the opening from Siobhan, not far from where Bok and Trinidad ended up, so she was able to see the Boatswain give the thumbs up.

And that was that. Nothing the defenders could do now.

Hand signals conveyed readiness to everyone, bodies pressed flat against the cold, gray hull.

In space, there is no atmosphere to convey sound, nor to diffract light and create shadows. Bok pressed a button on a comm attached to his belt, and all that changed.

Heather felt the sharp double-spike in the hand she had resting against the hull.

A moment later, air began to rush out of the airlock opening, where Bok and friends had attached explosive charges to both the outer and inner doors to destroy them.

She could imagine death-pressure warnings going off all over the crew sections of the vessel, followed by airlocks slamming tight to keep the ship from depressurizing. How paranoid the crew was would determine the next phase.

If they were lazy, they might have immediately tripped every airlock, dividing the crew into small chunks, separated by frames from each other, and possibly isolating them from suits. Heather could imagine how frightening it would be to wake up to pressure alarms and be trapped in your cabin.

Those people, however, would be the safest from what was coming. They were no threat to anyone.

Trinidad went back into the hole first. From the curves in the fieldsuit, the next figure had to be Nakisha Onks, although holding Dunklin's homemade grenade-rocket-gun would have also been a giveaway.

Siobhan went next, followed by the other four marines, Bok, and the rest of the boarders, in that sequence.

Heather counted bodies and cleared the outside of the ship, entering last. She had the least experience with something like this, compared to many ahead of her, and having her at the back put command officers at both ends of the snake.

At some point, Siobhan expected someone to come up from behind them.

Inside, beyond the destroyed airlock, she found a large room filled with EVA suits of various flavors for the crew. All were locked down and attached to the bulkheads, out of the way but easily accessible for someone just entering or just leaving the now-shattered airlock behind her.

"Blow the next hatch hard," Siobhan's voice came over the comm somewhat thin and attenuated. Low power beam, inside rugged, metal walls. "Keep them away from these suits unless they go into another airlock and then come back."

"Everyone take cover," Markus Dunklin hollered over the radio.

Heather stepped back into the airlock and to one side, hiding behind the solid walls. Another breach was imminent, and things would be flying around at high speed, especially trying to get by her into the cold vacuum outside.

"Three, two, one, go," came the call, followed on the last beat by another earthquake quivering through the hull.

Snowfall was suddenly rushing past her like a blizzard, air

and humidity flash frozen and expelled. It lasted for several seconds, and then fell to nothing.

Another chunk of the ship gutted open, like a fish. Nobody not currently in a suit would be able to get here and get into one, until the outer breach was covered or repaired.

Catch-22. For them.

"Moving," Trinidad called. "Lead team, close it up."

Heather hadn't bothered to draw her pistol before now. She was a good enough marksman, but had known there wouldn't be anything she needed to shoot at, especially not with this many armed marines around.

She drew it now, more as a symbol of authority than anything. Her job was aft coverage until something came along, with Dedra Janowski and Vlad Faurot, one of the marines, assisting her.

"Stairwell located," Trinidad called. "It's locked."

"Manual override on this one," Siobhan's hard voice replied. "Keep integrity at this point."

"Prybar," Bok ordered loudly.

Heather stole a glance to see a suited figure telescope out a metal rod and wedge it into a wheel lock at the base of the wall next to the door. In a complete power failure, you could always open a sealed hatch by turning the manual override. The area beyond it would vent, just as the previous ones had, but then they could seal it up again behind them and proceed, eventually remaining in pressure.

Locked hatches were a far sight easier to open if both sides read some level of pressure. But it also meant that the ship's crew could get at them easier.

Heather shifted herself a little closer to the middle of the column, tapping Vlad and pointing at the airlock behind them so he would be aimed at anyone who had somehow managed to suit up, sneak all the way across the width of the hull, and was trying to come up behind them.

Nobody was that fast right now, but given time, someone might have a clue.

Heather wanted to look at the corridor running parallel to the spine of the ship. It ran forward from here for a considerable distance, before ending in a wall. From her memory on the approach, that would possibly be another airlock, into the humongous ribcage where all the cargo containers were stored. Engineers would need access to them while docked.

"Dedra, assume an airlock at the end of that corridor," Heather said quietly. "Shoot anything that moves and call for help immediately, so they can't flank us."

"Yes, sir," the engineer replied, shifting her big bulk against a frame in such a way that her head and arm would be all that was visible.

Heather glanced forward. Prybar man was working, but the door was slowly moving.

"Stand by for pressure breach," Bok called.

Heather found a good place to be out of the way and grabbed on. The stairwell should have sealed horizontally at each deck, so there ought to be only a little air escaping.

Unless some idiot had overridden the locks, and the whole column of air was about to escape. She had seen dumber things in her career.

Those were usually terminal mistakes in space.

Puff of air suddenly riming into frost on the opening, but not that much. Just a single room opening to space.

"Lead team in," Siobhan ordered. "Prybar with them. Assume the same up a level. Open one more and then we'll feed in behind you."

The man next to the prybar reached into the bulkhead and manually locked the door against closing, at least for now. Nobody on the bridge could override, if they were lucky.

She corrected herself in that assumption, realizing that she was used to *Aquitaine*, and to a much lesser degree, *Fribourg*. *Buran* might not follow the standards of naval architecture Heather took for granted.

Nothing moved in her area of coverage, though. Lead team was talking on a different channel from everyone else right now, so they could chatter constantly, but not distract.

Something shuddered under Heather's feet, the whole hull rippling strangely. It took her a moment to identify the feeling.

The ship had just jumped.

That was the transition to JumpSpace. She wondered if they had triggered a blind jump forward, onto their next expected coordinates, or managed a reciprocal, and put themselves on a course that would return them to *Laptev*.

Not that something like that would help. They would still be at least another jump down to the friendly coverage of the guns on the station. Possibly two jumps, unless they got extremely lucky.

Still, risks. The clock was very much ticking, one way or the other.

"All hands," Heather said, just in case anyone had missed it. "The freighter is now in JumpSpace."

Dedra looked around just enough to grin and nod. The rest remained silent.

Out of their control now.

"Second level breach imminent," Battenhouse's voice came over the comm.

So, they had gotten up a level safely, and finished that process. More air and life was about to bleed out of the ship. More people trapped and watching their air reserves dwindle.

"All hands, move up to the stairwell," Siobhan ordered. "Heather, you'll have the bottom until we clear the top."

"Acknowledged, Siobhan," Heather said.

All the others columned into the stairwell quickly, leaving the room empty but for the three of them. Heather tapped Vlad first, and sent him back, followed by Dedra when Vlad was set.

It was a game of retrograde, armed leapfrog, as the three of them backed into the stairwell. Bok was there with the prybar close by. Probably a second prybar, so that the other engineer could go forward, as soon as this door sealed.

"Last in, Chief," Heather said.

Bok nodded and grabbed the wheel in the wall with both hands and began to spin it quickly, grunting with the effort of overcoming the weight of the door and any ice that had frozen in the track.

There was nothing Heather and her people could do but point guns out the rapidly-closing hatch, but the Boatswain had it closed much faster than Heather thought possible.

With a thump she felt in the soles of her feet, the hatch sealed. Bok rose, grabbed the prybar from the floor, and wedged it into the wheel and set the other end under the first stair.

Nobody was opening that wheel from the other side with it in place. Easier to just blow the entire bulkhead apart with explosives.

"Rear door secured," Bok called at he turned and attacked the stairs. Those people on the stairs themselves had pressed tight to one side to let the man through.

Heather nodded and waited for things to clear.

From here on in, there wasn't much she could do.

# HOGAN'S ALLEY (JUNE 5, 402)

THEY WERE past the point of *Lights! Camera! Action!* at this point, but Trinidad still felt a subtle change come over things as the sounds of Bok sealing the hatch below echoed up the column of the stairwell. Still, the helmet lights were on, just in case, and the camera was picking everything up so they could do a good after-action review for training.

You got better by studying what you did wrong the last time.

Up until now, every breach had meant people on the other side of a wall had to suddenly scramble for helmets at a dead minimum, on the way to getting into a pressurized suit of some sort so they didn't freeze and rupture. Now, the playing field would be leveled. Defending crew would be able to shoot at them rather than merely run because they had no air to breathe. And they could hold a defensive posture, assuming firearms.

For the very first time, it dawned on Trinidad that there might not be any guns on this ship. Or maybe, one or two, in case a crewman went nuts and needed to be stunned insensible. The ship had no naval guns. No civilian ship in *Buran*'s space had weapons.

And here he was, leading an armed insurrection, with five more guns than crew members on his side, when you took into account stunners, spares, and the pistol Nakisha had to go with her grenade launcher.

Still, he kept his opinions to himself. Better to be overarmed and perhaps overwhelm unarmed defenders, than to presume a flock of sheep who suddenly turned into wolves. As point man, he would be the first to encounter hostile fire.

"Markus, you ready?" he called over the comm, glancing down three steps to where Nakisha had an assault grenade in one hand, a pistol in the other, and the satchel of rockets with the launcher strung across her back.

"Say the word," the big engineer replied.

Somewhere below them, Bok would be climbing stairs as fast as those sixty-year-old legs would go in gravity, but they were racing the clock and defenders now. Bok could catch up.

"Go," Trinidad ordered, aiming his own pistol at the space where the hatch would open from the wall.

The wheel started to turn in Markus's hands, and then rolled back as soon as he let go.

"Damn it," the engineer growled. "Someone on the other side fighting me. Hang on."

Trinidad stepped back as the big man grabbed the prybar and wedged it into the spokes of the shin-level steel wheel. He turned it now by putting his entire weight against the end, until the prybar clanged loudly against the deck.

"Gerry, grab that wheel and hold it in place," Trinidad ordered.

Gerry was certainly not the brightest marine, but he was among the strongest. He lumbered over and grabbed one of the spokes in both hands, pulling up so hard that it actually turned another half-spin when whoever was on the other side suddenly lost their footing.

Markus jammed the prybar in quickly and turned, setting up a rhythm with Gerry, while Trinidad watched.

As a thought, Trinidad swapped the pulse pistol for the stunner he had in a pouch. Not particularly effective in vacuum, and extremely short ranged, compared to a pulse pistol, but they were in a stairwell that went up a level and ran into another hatch. You had to open it, pivot around a central post one hundred and eighty degrees, and then climb to the next hatch. Best way to seal between levels, and still let people move.

He turned to Nakisha and caught her eye, holding up the stunner and pointing it at the assault grenade in her hand.

"As soon as you can shove it through, okay?" he ordered.

She nodded and grinned. That girl was crazy, even by marine standards. One of these days, he'd have to get her a job as a stuntwoman, when they were all civilians again.

The hatch opened a crack. Not much, and it was moving a millimeter at a time as the people on the other side fought, but they were losing ground steadily to the prybar and the big marine.

Trinidad leaned in and fired the stunner through the gap. Not at anything, and probably couldn't hurt even if he did, but he wanted them skittish on the other side of the wall.

Sure enough, the wheel suddenly spun faster as someone lost a grip, or fell over, or something. Trinidad was able to get the barrel into the opening enough to get an angle on the next shot. He fired three jolts as quickly as the trigger would cycle.

Nakisha tapped him on the shoulder and Trinidad jumped back as she pushed her deadly egg into the gap. A moment later, the far side erupted in light and shockwave as the grenade went off.

Trinidad looked down and saw Gerry spinning the wheel freely now, all resistance stunned for a bit.

The door opened faster. Trinidad got an arm through enough to fire towards the defenders. There was someone there, holding his head and his ears. Trinidad put a shot dead center and watched the man collapse.

Footsteps sounding on the stairs caught his attention. Someone else was running up another level.

Trinidad bolted.

Marines ran up and down staircases in full gravity with heavy packs regularly, just so they could do something like this. He raced up two steps at a time, trusting his instincts to find the treads as his eyes stayed up to spot movement. From the sound, Nakisha wasn't far behind him.

He knew they were supposed to stay together. Boarding tactics stressed again and again the importance of not sallying so far ahead of your support that you got cut off. But he had Nakisha with him, and all her grenades and rockets. Siobhan could catch up. He might have the rest of the team out-gunned right now. Hell, maybe the rest of the ship.

The next turn of the stairs were there, and Trinidad saw a hatch slowly closing, faster than he could get there.

Damn it.

"Nakisha, hit them now," he yelled in desperation, watching whoever it was escape as the walls came together.

First rule of the new toy Markus had dreamt up for them: Rocket fuel is a pretty good smoke screen, as long as it doesn't set you on fire going by.

Had Trinidad not been in a combat suit, he might be *on fire* right now. Anybody but Nakisha taking that shot would have gotten an ass-chewing and possibly been disrated on all weapons until they requalified under a picky rangemaster.

The kind who owed Trinidad favors and could repay by making a marine's existence a living hell for a few weeks.

But this was First-Rate-Spacer Onks. And he had asked for it.

She hadn't missed his head by more than about six centimeters, but that was as good as a light year under these circumstances.

The angle of the shot was bad, going up the stairwell and hitting the ceiling of the space beyond through the gap, but the ensuing explosion was impressive. Smoke billowed back into the stairwell as something caught fire.

Second rule of rocket-propelled grenades in confined spaces: Splash damage is a bitch.

"What was that?" Trinidad asked as he took the last three steps at once and threw himself at the manual override wheel. The opening was only about ten centimeters right now.

"Fragmentation," she said. "Figured if I needed this one in a hurry, that would be the default, because using an assault or a wall-buster would have meant a slow situation."

Nobody was trying to finish closing the door. Trinidad held it in place for now with the override wheel, trying to see anything through the smoke.

"Two assault into the room, and then we'll go in," he ordered, wired like a squirrel with a double cappuccino.

She flipped the launcher over her shoulder again and pulled two gray-black eggs from pouches on the front of her suit.

"Fire in the hole," she yelled, shoving them through and drawing her pistol.

Twin hammerblows of light and sound a second later.

"Stunners only," Trinidad yelled over the roaring as she started to fire through the gap.

She paused and looked at him like he had lost his mind, but her training held. She drew the stunner with her left hand and stuck her whole arm through the opening, firing from left to right completely blind.

Trinidad focused on spinning the wheel. Gerry was suddenly there, hip-checking Trinidad politely out of the way and increasing the spin. Trinidad rose and drew his own stunner.

Nakisha peeked into the room and lobbed another assault grenade, nodding at her boss with an evil grin.

They had trained too much together, but that wasn't a bad thing. He knew she was going to tumble herself out into the room headed left, so he would need to cover the right side.

The next grenade went off.

Nakisha started her roll. Trinidad surged right after her.

Gravity failed, and the lights sputtered, dropping everything to nearly darkness, but for emergency lights.

Nakisha's graceful acrobatic spin ended up with her flailing in the air until she managed to grab a desk as she went by, watching her pistol fly out of her holster and then bounce off the far wall and head back. Trinidad tried to do the same, but missed grabbing the door as he went by and floated loosely in the direction of the far ceiling. He did retain his stunner.

And he was more or less upside down, looking at the room from above.

Smoke.

Well, a soft haze. Something electrical on fire.

Several somethings on fire, actually. The fire suppression system had apparently taken the first hit, and was spewing foam into the air, but not onto the three consoles that had apparently taken direct hits from something else.

Something moved behind a desk. A pulse of light blew past him just below his head with enough force and heat that he felt it.

Trinidad shot back on instinct, twisting like a worm on a hook. Marines trained to storm ships in the dark with strobes, to mimic the worst situations. You got your boarding cert when you could do it automatically.

"We surrender," a voice yelled moments later, over the sounds of fire, foam, and Nakisha's cursing as she tried to cover everything with a pulse pistol while tracking her other pistol so nobody else grabbed it.

Hands were in the air. Fearful eyes peeked over counters as Trinidad managed to get a boot magnet to lock himself to the roof, and then the second. Hopefully, they wouldn't suddenly turn the gravity back on, or he'd have to test if marines always landed on their feet.

There was no way in hell he would have the time to react.

"Come out," he answered in Mongolian, just so they heard and understood.

Five people in the room, floating. It looked like a bridge. Felt like one, anyway. One that had suffered a plague of angry pirates. They were holding on with their feet.

A sixth had been stunned and was hanging in a fetal curl not far from Trinidad.

A seventh had apparently been too close to the first grenade that had come into the room. He had been opened up like a knife slash, with fresh blood pooling on various surfaces before the gravity failed, now sticking instead. At least he had been dead when power failed. Trinidad had seen how much fun it could be to clean up a bubble of fresh blood floating in zero-g.

None of the crew members had life suits. Trinidad and his maniacs could have just blown locks open until they vented everyone to space without any risk.

But that wasn't the reputation he wanted to have. Nor Siobhan.

Speaking of which.

"Siobhan, this is Trinidad," he called. Three seconds had passed since Nakisha entered the room. "Bridge appears secure."

"On my way," she replied.

On an outside line, he continued talking.

"Where is your captain?" he asked.

Blank looks. Not captain. Weirdoes did that wrong, too.

"Where is your director?" he fixed his vocabulary and challenged the closest one.

Fearful hands pointed at the man Trinidad had shot.

Made sense. Only the commander probably had access to what might be the only firearm on the ship. At least before today.

"What's the situation?" Siobhan called as she entered.

Trinidad grinned at her, cognizant of all the smoke, fire, and death around them.

"Need a couple of engineers to fix things," he said. "And a pilot to do some of her navigating magic, but I appear to have captured you a freighter."

"Excuse me?" Nakisha barked. "You weren't alone, you know."

At that moment, somewhere below, an engineer managed to fix a shorted line, or reroute a damaged trunk, and the grav-plates suddenly came back on, full power.

Trinidad plummeted two meters to the deck with a howl of surprise, clanging his helmet like someone throwing an anvil down a staircase.

Gerry, the big dumb marine, was standing in the doorway where his helmetcam would have the best view, next to Siobhan when Trinidad looked up.

"And PRINT!" the big marine yelled.

# PACKMULE (JUNE 8, 402)

Siobhan felt like the cat with all the best cream in the refrigerator, just awaiting her pleasure. The big freighter had been easy enough to move, once they'd hijacked it. *Laptev* had no coast guard or naval forces capable of chasing them across space, so she had just programmed a course for the Gulf and jumped.

Best to lead the locals astray, as the second jump had been sideways and down, and then down again, until they passed all the way around *Laptev* and ended up fifty-some light years closer to *Severnaya Zemlya* than they started. Not too close, as Phil had expected heightened patrols, after what Keller and crew had done last time, but the last place anybody would look for them.

The new conference room was packed with friendly bodies. Siobhan was on the second prize with most of the officers, plus Bok representing the crew. The ship had a number: long, messy, and impersonal, but everyone had taken to calling it *Packmule*, on account of it being slow, balky, stubborn, and being able to haul an impossible amount of food around.

Julius Gephardt, *Jules*, was just finishing up his rundown of the inventory they had eventually pried out of the computers.

Phil interrupted with a waved hand as Jules started off on another tangent that included gumbo ala king, which sounded rather awesome to Siobhan. She would have liked to see where that went, but Phil was in charge.

"Boil it down," Phil grumbled. "Give me numbers, and not recipes."

Siobhan nearly laughed at the look of thwarted genius that flashed across the Chef's face for the briefest moment. She wondered how hard the man was fighting not to eyeroll his own command centurion.

"Fine," Jules huffed after a moment. "Assuming the usual rate of spoilage, waste, and shrinkage as we have maintained for the last two years, we have roughly nineteen and a half months' worth of food stocks, between the three vessels. Siobhan got lucky, in that *Laptev* doesn't grow oats, so they had just delivered their last stores of that grain to the surface, replacing it with something genetically close to Russian Red Number Two wheat. Now all I need are chickens."

"Chickens, Jules?" Phil was lost. But the man never cooked. Xui Yi, his wife, was a fantastic chef, and had entertained Siobhan and Heather for dinner on a couple of occasions, before *CS-405* went to the far ends of the galaxy.

"I need fresh eggs, Phil," Jules said. "We've got the grain, the water, and the milk. With eggs, I can make dumplings, gnocchi, bread, and any pasta you want. But I need chickens."

He turned to Siobhan with a deadly serious face.

"Alive, this time, by the way," Jules continued.

That got a tremendous laugh from all the way around the room. Everybody had enjoyed the fresh chicken, and then discovering bone broth after that had been a double win.

But yeah, they would need chickens. Siobhan could see that. Possibly cows, too, if they wanted fresh milk on a regular basis.

Phil rubbed a big paw down his face, as if trying to wipe away the weirdness of the day. They had gotten away. And stolen one of the biggest cargo vessels in the sector, fully loaded with goods. And enough food to stay at sea for a *long* time, since the Expeditionary Corvette was designed with exactly that in mind.

"Are you suggesting we hit a farming world next?" Phil finally asked, right up at the edge of exasperated.

Jules shrugged and gave everyone his best, awesomist chef's sneer.

"You want to continue to eat like kings and queens, I need a better logistics train," he scolded. "Think of it as trading up for other problems. You won't starve. Now you'll bitch about needing a fancier menu instead."

More laughter.

"We can't hold a planet," Phil groused.

"We don't have to, Phil," Siobhan finally spoke up, unable to contain the mad energy in her belly much longer. Or the giggles. "Why not take one they don't know about?"

Heather, of all people, turned a hard eye on Siobhan.

"Stop reading my mind, Siobhan," the First Officer challenged.

"What are you two up to?" Jules asked, possibly frightened that the women were about to call his bluff.

"We know what systems *Buran* claims," Siobhan replied. "We have their entire navigational records for the sector."

"Correct," Heather took up the thread now. "And there must be worlds that just haven't been colonized yet. Look how many planets the ancients terraformed in the early days. Let's steal one."

"Steal a planet?" Phil asked, his voice heavy with sarcastic disbelief.

"Hey, finders keepers, right?" Siobhan countered. "And we are a scout. Let's become explorers."

Siobhan noted a change in Phil's eyes when she said that. Must have triggered something, because the man suddenly smiled.

"Yes," he agreed, maybe a little too readily. "But a farm needs farmers. Either you folks take up tilling the soil, or we're going to have to get someone else to do it. And I'm not about to go capture prisoners, just to make them work."

"We've got twenty-nine warm bodies now," Siobhan offered.

"Twenty-seven," Heather corrected her. "Kiel and Lan are passengers, not prisoners."

"Do they know anybody?" Siobhan asked, more as a joke than anything.

She grew concerned when Phil's face got serious. Like maybe he was considering asking them if they had cousins interested in starting a farm somewhere.

"I'll ask," he said after a beat. "What's the worst they could say? No?"

"Wait," Siobhan was aghast. "Serious? Get some folks from *The Holding* and ask them to run a secret farm for us on an unknown planet? That sort of thing?"

"Fresh start on a new world," Heather, of all people mused. "Plus a lot of free labor from us, setting them up in the first place so they can become self-sufficient. I imagine you could be rather successful, if you didn't have any capital loans to pay off, and no taxman coming."

"What have you crazy bastards been up to while Trinidad and I have been off having adventures?" Siobhan asked sarcastically.

"Plotting how to get even," Evan Brinich suddenly spoke up. "Oatmeal was right out, so we had to get creative."

More laughter. Siobhan grinned. It was good to be home.

"Okay," Phil tapped a finger on the table top to get everyone's attention. "This sounds like something worth investigating. Who knows anything about farms? I'm a city boy."

"You know," the Boatswain suddenly spoke up. "I've been giving some thought to retiring from the Navy for a while now. This might be a good job for me."

"What do you know about tilling the soil, Bok?" Phil asked. "You've been in the fleet longer than most of the rest of us have been alive."

"And before that, I grew up milking cows and mucking out stables twice a day," the short man replied. "Joined the Navy to get as far from that life as possible. That's why I've stayed in for forty-three years. But I could see retiring to a farm. Actually, it would be more of a secret naval base than anything else."

"How much crew would you need?" Phil turned his whole torso to face his Boatswain. "To do it right?"

"Assuming you can hit a farm somewhere and steal chickens and other livestock?" Bok asked. "Surprisingly few. Most of the work we can automate, so we'll need tractors and pumps for the most part. Bodies are necessary when it comes time to harvest."

"Start a list," Phil ordered, taking Siobhan's breath away. "That will tell me who we need to hit next."

Phil Kosnett was serious. They weren't going to take the *Packmule* and *Queen Anne's Revenge* and just run across the border for home. He was looking at going full-on pirate, raiding *Buran* space for a living, or at least until they could get a message to Keller or the Imperials.

Imperials.

"Hey," Siobhan asked suddenly, cutting off all the chatter as heads turned towards her. "Does anyone know what *Buran* does with Imperial prisoners they take, after a ship is lost attacking *Samara*? I don't see *The Eldest* just hauling them out back and shooting them. Goes against most of what that bastard professes to believe about what's best for humanity. Where do they go?"

Dead silence. Quizzical faces and shrugs.

"Would there be anything in the logs of the *Packmule*?" Heather asked. "The ship goes to dozens of planets. I've never looked in the Gazetteer for something like that, but nobody ever asked. *Fribourg* and *Aquitaine* always had a channel for swapping people home after a year or so."

"You and Siobhan find out," Phil ordered fiercely. "That's a labor force we can use, as well as a marine raiding company we can train, if they exist and we can find them. Ladies and gentlemen, understand this. We could make it home right now, safe and sound and extremely successful with the two ships we've captured and the damage we've done to *Buran*. I'm not satisfied, however. Keller will have to regroup and repair ships, so *Buran* would have time to do the same. I don't intend to give them that time. We can keep up the pressure here, and harass the hell out of this entire sector, and the ones around it, just by continuing to act like pirates. We need a base next, and then it will be time to consider if we should leave the Caribbean and sail to North America, South America, Africa, or hit prime targets in Spain and France."

He paused, slowly turning his head to fix his gaze on everyone. Siobhan felt the mad power in those eyes as he got to her.

"The rest of Keller's squadron always gets the combat glory," Phil said. "I intend to do something here that will rank up there with *The Long Raid* and *The Expedition*. Any questions?"

Siobhan held her breath. So did the rest of them.

The audacity of what Phil Kosnett was proposing made everything she had done up until now look like knocking over a corner convenience store for pocket change.

Siobhan found Heather's eyes, seated on the other side of Phil. They shared a hard, meaningful smile, flashing back to the captured bridge of this ship, and the potential for mischief they had discussed.

And now, Phil was going to top that.

"I'm in," Heather said simply.

"Let's do this," *Lady Blackbeard* answered her.

# ABOUT THE AUTHOR

Blaze Ward writes science fiction in the Alexandria Station universe (Jessica Keller, The Science Officer, The Story Road, etc.) as well as several other science fiction universes, such as Star Dragon, the Collective, and more. He also writes odd bits of high fantasy with swords and orcs. In addition, he is the Editor and Publisher of *Boundary Shock Quarterly Magazine.* You can find out more at his website www.blazeward.com, as well as Facebook, Goodreads, and other places.

Blaze's works are available as ebooks, paper, and audio, and can be found at a variety of online vendors (Kobo, Amazon, and others). His newsletter comes out quarterly, and you can also follow his blog on his website. He really enjoys interacting with fans, and looks forward to any and all questions—even ones about his books!

**Never miss a release!**
If you'd like to be notified of new releases, sign up for my newsletter.

I will never spam you or use your email for nefarious purposes. You can also unsubscribe at any time.

http://www.blazeward.com/newsletter/

**Connect with Blaze!**

Web: www.blazeward.com
Boundary Shock Quarterly (BSQ):
https://www.boundaryshockquarterly.com/

facebook.com/KRPBlaze

goodreads.com/Blaze_Ward

# ABOUT KNOTTED ROAD PRESS

Knotted Road Press fiction specializes in dynamic writing set in mysterious, exotic locations.

Knotted Road Press non-fiction publishes autobiographies, business books, cookbooks, and how-to books with unique voices.

Knotted Road Press creates DRM-free ebooks as well as high-quality print books for readers around the world.

With authors in a variety of genres including literary, poetry, mystery, fantasy, and science fiction, Knotted Road Press has something for everyone.

Knotted Road Press
www.KnottedRoadPress.com